Daughter of the Dispossessed

J.L. Henker

DEDICATION

This novella is dedicated to the members of Women Writing Other Worlds—An Alliance of Women Fantasy & Science Fiction Authors. This amazing group of women provided the support and encouragement that made this work possible.

Book Cover Design: 100Covers.com

Maps: Barney2147 (Fiverr.com)

Editor: Sarah Ramos

For information contact:
jlhenkerauthor@gmail.com
https://jlhenker.com

CONTENTS

CONTENT WARNING

The following elements are briefly mentioned in some chapters: animal injury, emotional abuse of a child, sexual innuendo, bondage, and blood.

NORTHERN WILDS

KINGDOM OF SIGOR

GUNDERVELT MOUNTAINS

ALGOWIN

DRAGONSWOLD

EDGEWATER

N
E
S

THE GREAT LAKE

DRAGONSBACK MOUNTAINS

SIGOR CITY

THE BAY OF SIGOR

IMPERIUM

SHANDGALAH MOUNTAINS

SOUTHERN DESERT

SORATHAN

CHAPTER ONE
CHILD OF THE FOREST

M oss-covered planks creaked and groaned as Lord Gabrian stepped onto the porch. He shoved open the door of the tiny cabin with his boot and recoiled from the smell of dirty clothes, old cooking oil, and moldy straw. Twilight filtered through two dirty windows, and a candle flickered on a roughly hewn table. A man and a woman dressed in rags trembled in the shadows.

"Where's the child?" Gabrian asked.

The man gestured to a girl with pale skin and white hair, hunched over blankets on the floor. Gabrian pierced them with a furious glare. "This is how you treat a child gifted with magic?"

The couple retreated even farther into the corner, afraid to speak.

Gabrian took a threatening step forward. "Answer me!"

"She's been nothing but a curse." The cowering man raised his shoulders and stepped forward. "We should have left the halfling to the forest demons."

Gabrian grabbed the edge of the table and shoved it aside. The candle and holder crashed to the floor, its light fizzling out. He lurched forward and seized the man by his collar. "You ignorant churl. You should pray to whatever god you believe in that I don't tie you up and leave you in the forest for the wolves."

He released the man, wiped his hands on his cloak, and threw a bag of coins onto the dusty floor. "It's more than you deserve. Consider yourselves lucky to be alive."

Gabrian walked over to the child and knelt.

Her eyes grew wide, and she scooted deeper into the corner.

"What's your name?"

She pulled a blanket onto her lap.

He extended his hand. "I won't hurt you."

The girl placed her palm in his. Her magic shimmered, raw and uncontrolled.

Gabrian smirked. His source had been right about the strange child at the forest's edge.

"Won't you tell me your name?"

"Ayleth," she whispered.

"That's lovely. How old are you?"

"Six."

Gabrian stood, pulled her from the floor, and felt her ribs through the thin cotton shift. He turned to her parents and scowled. "This child is starving."

"She refuses to eat what we give her." The man glared at Gabrian. "She goes out into the forest and eats bugs; the gods know what else."

Gabrian shifted his attention to the woman huddled behind her husband. "What do you have to say? Are you her mother?"

She shook her head and pointed toward the trees outside the window. "A baby was crying, and I searched for it. Someone abandoned her beneath a tree, and I feared the wolves would eat her, so I brought her home."

"I told her to take the unnatural thing back and leave her to the forest creatures, but she refused," her husband grumbled.

Gabrian's nostrils flared. "You let her languish here instead of finding someone to teach her?"

The woman stepped forward. "I felt she was special." She glanced over her shoulder. "But he..."

The man balled his fists. "Shut up, woman."

"Enough!" Gabrian glared at them. "You rescued the child. For that kindness, I'll spare you." He approached the door and glanced over his shoulder. "Tell no one where she's gone. If anyone asks, she disappeared into the forest."

They nodded.

The cabin door opened, and Gabrian's Marshall of the Guard, Cassian, stuck his head in. "Is everything alright, sir?"

"No!" Gabrian pushed past Cassian with the child in his arms.

"What about them?" Cassian pointed at the man and woman.

"Leave them. Tell your men to mount up." Gabrian walked out the door.

Cassian stepped off the porch and motioned to his two guards.

Eadric and Johan stood at attention by the horses.

"You heard him. Mount up."

Gabrian marched toward his horse, and his boot struck something. He peered at a pile of tiny bones scattered across the forest floor.

Ayleth squirmed to free herself from his grasp.

Gabrian let her slide to the ground.

She gathered the scattered pieces and reverently placed them in a pile.

Johan pointed towards the trees. More bones were hanging in strands that twirled in the breeze.

Gabrian extended his hand. "Ayleth, come with me and leave those."

She fussed with the bone cache, arranging them in an order that made sense only to her.

"Come. Now." Gabrian frowned.

She picked up a small animal skull and clasped it to her chest.

Eadric and Johan exchanged glances.

Gabrian turned to Eadric and motioned to Ayleth. "Eadric. Wrap her up and keep her warm. She'll ride with you."

"I'm not cold," Ayleth said.

His brow wrinkled. "We want you to be comfortable. It's a long journey."

Ayleth nodded.

Gabrian picked her up and tucked her into the saddle in front of Eadric.

"We'll travel for a few hours before we stop to rest and eat," Gabrian said. "We don't want to draw attention to ourselves."

Ayleth stared at Gabrian. "I'm not hungry."

A slight grin appeared at the corner of Gabrian's lips. "That's good, Ayleth. Though my men will grow hungry soon. You don't have to eat unless you want to."

Eadric glanced back at the bones dangling from the trees and turned to Johan. "I've seen something like that once before in the borderlands to the north. They warned outsiders to stay away."

Johan stared at the bones and shivered.

Eadric turned away from the strange offerings and glanced from Ayleth to Johan. "It's rumored that those who ignored them never returned."

Ayleth hummed an unearthly tune.

The hair on the back of Eadric's neck stood up.

Cassian and Gabrian rode in front of Eadric. Johan guarded their flank. Gabrian turned in the saddle to study the strange child with wide eyes and matted hair. *What was her heritage?* There were tales of demon-like beings with white hair and skeletal forms that inhabited the most remote edges of the northern forests. He had dismissed them as stories to frighten children and drunken soldiers. He frowned. The child had unusual magic, and its texture gave him an idea of where she acquired it. If he were right, he had spent his gold well.

Ayleth fidgeted, pointed toward some trees, and grunted.

"What is it?" Eadric asked.

She squirmed and tried to slide off.

He pulled back on the reins. "Hold on. I'll help you down. We can take a break."

When her feet hit the ground, she hurried into the trees.

Eadric followed but stopped when he heard her relieving herself. He blushed and turned around.

"Don't go far," Gabrian said. "I'll always know where to find you."

She emerged from the forest and approached Eadric's horse to stroke his neck. A slight smile creased her lips.

Gabrian motioned to Ayleth. "Are you hungry yet?"

Ayleth nodded and sat down in the dirt.

Gabrian held out his hand. "Get up and come over here. Do not sit on the ground anymore. Do you understand?"

She nodded again and perched next to him on a fallen log.

Gabrian placed a bag beside her and pulled out some cheese and chunks of bread. "Would you like some?"

Ayleth perused the food in his hand, scrunched up her nose, and looked back toward the trees.

"Listen to me, Ayleth." Gabrian frowned. "You will eat what we give to you or go hungry."

Her eyes narrowed. "But..."

He put the food into her hand. "It's this or nothing."

Ayleth sniffed the piece of cheese. She hesitated, then placed it on her tongue and sat straighter. She grabbed a bigger piece and shoved it into her mouth, along with a piece of bread, swallowed, and stared at Gabrian. "More?"

After Ayleth finished eating, they remounted. She slumped forward, and her eyes drooped with exhaustion. Soon, she was breathing deeply.

Gabrian urged his mount to increase its pace. They rode all night and most of the following day, briefly stopping to eat and rest. At dusk, they arrived at a small forester's village at the base of the Gundervelt Mountains. A cozy inn tempted them, but Gabrian urged them on to Algowin.

Ayleth shifted back and forth in front of Eadric, glancing at men hurrying back to their humble cabins where candlelight flickered in the windows. There were more people than she had ever seen. Once the town disappeared, she settled against his chest.

Darkness enveloped them as they rode up the mountain toward Algowin.

Ayleth gasped and pointed at the lights in the keep's towers.

Gabrian smiled. "This is your new home."

They entered the central courtyard. Gabrian's assistant, Lenora, and his chief advisor, Bethyl, walked out from the keep to meet them.

Lenora spotted the child, and her eyebrows rose. She rushed forward and held out her hands. "Give her to me."

Eadric handed Ayleth down to Lenora's waiting arms.

She gasped. "What in Halia's name..."

Gabrian put his finger to his lips. "I'll tell you everything later. Get her washed and fed, then stay by her bed until she falls asleep."

Lenora nodded and hurried away with the child clasped firmly in her arms.

Bethyl watched Lenora disappear into the keep. "Is the child what you hoped for?"

Gabrian let out a slow breath. "Her magic is unlike anything I've ever encountered."

Bethyl rubbed her hands nervously. "Will you be able to control it?"

"We'll see," he said and hurried after Lenora.

Gabrian's fingers tapped on the wooden desktop as he gazed out the window of his study. *The child has otherworldly magic, but what kind?* He pursed his lips. Her energy vibrated through the stone walls of the keep, and he could sense her moving around. *Is she part god or part demon? Is she connected to dragon magic?*

A knock sounded on the door.

Gabrian looked up as Bethyl entered.

"Is she asleep?" he asked.

Bethyl nodded. "Finally. I had Lenora slip something into a cup of warm milk."

Gabrian raised an eyebrow. "Was she afraid?"

"No. Excited, I think." Bethyl stared at him and then shook her head. "Great gods, Gabrian. She is behaving like a starving animal. What about her parents?"

"I spared them," Gabrian sighed. "But they deserved to be drawn and quartered for allowing her to live under such conditions."

Bethyl sat down on the edge of a chair. "She's feral, but only because no one has worked with her."

Gabrian nodded. "I need you to teach her to be a proper young woman and how to control her magic."

Bethyl gestured toward her aging body and grey hair. "Do I look like someone's mother?"

The corner of Gabrian's mouth crept upward. "Grandmother, maybe."

She snorted. "I don't have a nurturing bone in my body. I dislike children even more than baby animals. They're noisy and uncontained."

"Then you both can learn something." Gabrian's brow furrowed.

Bethyl shook her head. "This is no normal child. There's something strange and powerful about her. Where did you say they found her?"

"Beneath a tree in the woods," Gabrian said.

Bethyl placed a hand over her heart. "Ludager's balls, Gabrian. She could be any sort of unnatural creature that looks like a child."

"Of course." Gabrian grinned. "That's why I went to fetch her."

Bethyl frowned. "Let Lenora take her on. I don't have the patience."

"You're the strongest mage here," Gabrian waved his hand, "besides me."

"Why don't you do it then?" She huffed.

Gabrian tilted his head. "Because I dislike children even more than you do."

Bethyl leaned in close to Gabrian and scowled. "It's a fool's errand. Why would you waste our time with the wraith?"

Gabrian briefly gazed out the window. "We must be ready."

"You've been telling me this for years." Bethyl shook her head. "I'll be dead and buried if something doesn't happen soon."

He closed his eyes, placed his hand on his brow, and touched the keep with his mind. Two floors down, magic stirred. "You should go. Ayleth's awake."

Bethyl's eyebrows rose. "How do you know?"

"I can sense it."

"I'll go, but I agree to nothing more." She stood up.

"You will do as I ask because I speak the truth." His lips pursed. "You want the dragons back as much as I do."

She gave him a piercing glare and left the room.

He poured himself a glass of wine and walked out onto his balcony. Streaks of clouds tinted red and purple illuminated the night sky. He sighed, gazing up toward the top of Mount Abarask, and imagined dragons encircling its majestic peak. *They would return. Soon.*

Chapter Two

DISCOVERING DRAGONS

Bethyl chased the naked girl around the bed and across the room. "Take a bath and get dressed!"

Ayleth shrieked and disappeared behind the thick drapery that covered the window.

Bethyl kicked the child's filthy slip that lay crumpled on the floor. "You can't run away from me forever. Come out and get in the tub. You'll feel much better once you've had a bath."

A tiny grunt echoed from behind the curtain.

"Once you wash and get dressed, we'll get something to eat," Bethyl said.

This time, there was a squeak.

Bethyl crept toward the curtain.

Ayleth bolted across the room and dove under the bed.

Bethyl groaned. *What could entice this child to comply?* She disappeared into the hallway and returned with a soft, fuzzy kitten. She set it on the ground by the edge of the bed, where it mewed pitifully.

Ayleth's head emerged.

"Would you like to pet the kitten?" Bethyl said, extending her arms.

A tiny hand reached for the soft bundle.

Bethyl scooped it away. "First you bathe, then the kitten."

The child slid out from under the bed. She stared at the kitten as she stepped sideways toward the steaming tub.

Bethyl nodded. "Good. Get in and scrub. Then you can hold her."

Ayleth tentatively put her hand into the warm water and lifted her leg over the edge, sliding in slowly. She splashed around and began to climb back out.

"Not yet," Bethyl shook her head. "Use soap and scrub everything, including your hair."

Ayleth dunked her head under the water and emerged, sputtering and spitting.

"Great gods, child." Bethyl crossed her arms. "Have you never had a proper bath?"

She glared at Bethyl and picked up the soap.

Bethyl checked Ayleth and nodded. "You can come out now." She held out a towel. "Get dry. Then you can hold the kitten."

Ayleth wiped herself quickly, dropped the towel, and held out her hands.

Bethyl handed her a clean shift. "Put this on."

She lifted it over her head and wiggled into it.

Bethyl handed her the kitten.

Ayleth squeezed it tightly and pushed it against her cheek.

Bethyl's eyes widened. "Be gentle. It's a baby."

She sat on the floor, held the kitten to her chest, and rocked back and forth. It started to squirm and cry. Ayleth's eyes widened. "What's wrong?"

"Don't worry," Bethyl held out her hand. "The kitty is hungry. Let me take her back to her mama."

Ayleth snuggled her face into the kitten's fur, sighed, and handed it to Bethyl.

"Good," Bethyl said. "Put on the leggings and shoes, and we'll go downstairs to eat."

"I'm not hungry." Ayleth scowled.

"You must eat." Bethyl turned toward the door and then glanced over her shoulder. "I'll be right back." She ducked into the hallway and deposited the kitten into the closet with its mother and littermates. She returned to the room and searched for Ayleth. *That child!*

Bethyl hurried down the stairs and entered the main foyer.

Ayleth squirmed in the arms of a guard, spitting and snarling like a bobcat.

Bethyl gritted her teeth and sent every swear word she could think of in Gabrian's direction.

A book flew across the room and knocked a lamp off the side table.

Ayleth stomped her foot. "I don't want to read anymore."

"Stop," Bethyl crossed her arms. "You'll do as I say."

She threw another book and bolted toward the door.

Bethyl groaned. She stood and lurched after her fleeing pupil. Her aching knees brought her to a halt. She flicked her fingers and flung a shimmering cord of magic.

Ayleth skidded to a stop, her arms bound securely to her sides.

Bethyl reined her in like a tethered sheep.

The child struggled and cursed.

"If you're going to act like a wild animal, I'll treat you like one." Bethyl cinched the restraint tighter.

"Let me go!" Ayleth hissed.

The mage ignored her pleas and conjured a metal cage several feet in diameter. She grabbed Ayleth by the arm and shoved her in, locking the metal latch with magic.

Ayleth threw herself against the bars.

"If you keep that up, you're going to hurt yourself." Bethyl stared at the child. "I'll be back later." She walked out and slammed the door.

Ayleth rattled the bars and shrieked.

A guard stationed outside the door glanced from Bethyl to the room. "Is everything in order?"

"No!" Bethyl stormed off down the hall.

Ayleth huddled in a ball on the floor. The balcony doors stood open, and a chilly evening breeze whistled into the room. She curled tighter into a ball and rubbed her arms for warmth. *I won't let the old hag win.* She gritted her teeth, sat up, and gazed around the dreary room. The grey stone walls were bare, except for several candle sconces by the front door and a tapestry of an old woman who wore a crown and a scowl. A brown quilt covered the bed, and the only color was her burgundy cape that hung on a peg by a rickety armoire. *I need to get outside!*

She stood and rubbed her hands together. Within moments, a familiar spark flashed between her palms. She focused her attention on a pile of blankets on the bed and sent a spark flying. Smoke billowed, and they burst into flames. She grinned and sat down to wait.

The guard rushed in and ran toward the bed. "Ludager's balls. Are you trying to kill yourself?" He threw a pitcher of water onto the flames, bundled the mess into a ball, and threw it off the balcony into the canyon below.

Bethyl stormed in and stood by the cage with her hands on her hips.

"Do you think I'll let you out now?" She turned to the guard. "Remove everything from the room."

He stared at Bethyl.

"Did you hear me?" Bethyl glared at him. "Get some help and get everything out. Now!"

He nodded and disappeared into the hallway. He returned with three other guards, who hauled the furniture away. The room was bare within an hour.

Ayleth whimpered.

Bethyl paced around the room. "There's nothing left to burn. What will you do now?"

Ayleth hung her head and stared at the floor.

Bethyl stopped pacing and arched an eyebrow. "You have two choices. Behave like a young woman or stay here caged like an animal."

"Let me out," Ayleth whispered.

"What?" Bethyl glared at her. "I didn't hear you."

"Let. Me. Out." Ayleth stood up and grabbed the bars of the cage.

Bethyl stepped closer. "You'll stay here a few days until you fully understand the privilege Gabrian offers you."

Ayleth scowled, and magic sparked in her palms.

"You have no power over me," Bethyl smirked and turned toward the door.

Ayleth flung her magic at the old mage's back and sent her crashing into the wall.

Ayleth fidgeted in an overstuffed chair in Gabrian's study. She studied the shelves full of books and walls covered in paintings of strange beings and battles.

"You will now study with me," Gabrian snapped his fingers. "You may not use magic without my permission. If you do, I'll make you wish you were back in your cage. Do you understand?"

She nodded her head.

"I'll help you learn to use your magic so you're never subjected to ridicule or abuse again." He paused momentarily. "That's my promise to you, and I require one in return."

Ayleth tilted her head. "What?"

"You'll pay attention and study hard. You cannot become a mage until you've mastered your magic." He cleared his throat and pointed to a painting on the wall. "Do you know what that is?"

She shook her head.

"It's a dragon." Gabrian's eyes narrowed. "We used to have many here."

"Like kittens?"

He frowned. "No, nothing like kittens. Come here, let me show you."

Gabrian lifted her onto a high stool and pulled out a piece of paper, a quill, and his inkwell. He placed all the items on his worktable and drew a tiny stick figure in the bottom corner of the parchment. "That's you," he said, pointing. His subsequent pen strokes filled the entire page with the image of a large winged creature like the one on the wall. "This is a dragon."

The child pondered the drawing, then gasped. "That's bigger than a horse."

"It is. Much."

Ayleth swiveled around on the stool and peered up at him. "Do you have one?"

His shoulders slumped forward. "No. But that's why you're here. You can help us find some.

She traced the figure with her finger and quivered. Ayleth gazed up at Gabrian. "Can I ride it?"

Gabrian's lips twitched. "Possibly, if we get the right ones."

She grinned.

Gabrian went over to a shelf behind his table, pulled off a large leather-bound volume, and placed it in front of Ayleth. "Here are pictures of the dragons that once lived at Algowin."

She gently turned the pages. "Where did they go?"

"That's a long story. You'll learn soon, I promise. For now, I need you to pay attention to your studies. There's much for you to learn before you can help me bring them home."

Ayleth turned a page of the book to a picture of a massive grey dragon soaring over mountaintops in the distance. She jerked upright. "Here?"

Gabrian nodded and held out his hand. "Come with me."

She clasped his fingers and slid to the floor. He guided them outside onto his balcony, which overlooked a grand gorge that swept down from the Gundervelt Mountains. He pointed to the highest mountaintop. "The dragon in the picture was soaring there. A long way to the east is a kingdom called Dragonswold. The dragons live there with the clever and devious Guardians. They stole the dragons from us a long time ago, and we wish to bring them back to Algowin."

Ayleth's eyes widened. "How do you steal a dragon?"

Gabrian leaned on the banister. "With powerful magic."

Ayleth craned her neck and peered at the mountain toward its highest peaks. "Do you think we can do it?"

"Yes," Gabrian said. "Do you want to help?"

Ayleth nodded.

Chapter Three
COMING OF AGE

Ayleth crouched over her worktable. A warm breeze crept into the room and stirred the bone mobile dangling above her. Animal skulls adorned the shelves, and a cluster of magic-infused crystals lay meticulously arranged in the corner. It had taken five years before Gabrian permitted her to wander the forest alone, and several more years to collect them all. The rocks, stones, and bones made her feel at home. She rubbed her eyes, focused on the parchment map in front of her, and traced the outline of the nearby mountains with her finger. A whisper of energy pulled her toward the peaks to the north. She shook her head and frowned. *I'll travel there someday to find out why.*

A soft knock at the door drew her attention.

Gabrian approached the table and looked down.

"Planning your escape?"

She rolled her eyes and pointed to the map. "Have you ever been there?"

He peered down and tapped. "Here. Just to the base of this crag. The weather worsened, and we had to turn back. Why?"

"Nothing important." She touched a finger to her lips.

His brow creased. "I've noticed it too."

Ayleth looked up. "What?"

Gabrian waved his hand around the room. "Your connection to earth energy, your love of rocks and bones."

Ayleth's hand touched the small skull she always carried in her pocket, its presence comforting.

"I've been studying the books you've given me since I was six. I still don't understand."

"Some mages can connect with diverse elements in the natural world. It's usually wind, water, and fire. Those are very common." Gabrian paused to contemplate. "Your magic is broader and deeper. What happens when you handle the bones?"

Ayleth pursed her lips and scowled. "It's like..." she paused and closed her eyes, "I can almost see them as if they're trying to tell me something, but I can't grasp the missing pieces."

Gabrian nodded. "It's ancient and connects you to a primitive magic that goes back to the beginning of time when the Unnamed Ones created everything."

She wrinkled her nose. "What does that mean?"

Gabrian smiled. "I've been waiting for the right time to show you something. I think you're ready."

"If it's another dusty book, I'll scream." Ayleth put her hands on her hips.

"It's not." He chuckled. "It's my prized possession, and I think you'll be very excited to see it."

Ayleth jumped off her stool and raced to the door. "Let's go."

"Very well." He followed her out. They went higher into the tower and stopped outside Gabrian's sleeping chamber. He opened the door and ushered her in.

She sucked a breath between her teeth. Gabrian had never allowed her in his most private space.

"Wait here." He stepped into the back corner behind a table, raised his hand, and murmured under his breath. Within moments, a door appeared. He opened it and motioned for Ayleth to follow.

She entered a darkened room with no windows. It smelled of candles and stale air. She jolted to a stop. That wasn't all. It reeked of bones. "What is this place?"

Mage lights flickered on in alcoves around the room, exposing a round table.

Gabrian pointed at something resting in the middle.

Ayleth squinted her eyes to see in the dim light. Her breath caught in her throat. It was a giant skull, unlike anything she had ever seen. The rows of massive teeth reminded her of a bear, but bigger. She moved closer, and the surrounding air stirred.

"Is it an ice bear?"

"No." He placed a hand over his heart. "Something much bigger. This is from a very young one."

Ayleth gasped. "This was a baby?"

Gabrian nodded. "Touch it."

She reached a trembling hand toward the skull. Her fingers brushed the cold bone, and sparks of energy rushed up her arm. Her brain exploded with images. Dragons soared through the air, snow sparkled on mountain peaks, and the Great Lake spread out below. The images vibrated with joy, freedom, and power.

Ayleth let go and scowled. "You killed a dragon?"

"No." He shook his head vigorously. "Dragon bones are scarce. They're so quick to burn their dead to ash that it's almost impossible to find one unless you slay a dragon in battle. Some treasure hunters discovered this one buried in the cellar of an abandoned keep in the Shandgalah Mountains to the south."

A whistle escaped her lips. "I can feel things with the other bones, but I've never had visions."

"Memories of the dragon's past lives remain locked in their bones. I can sense and work with the magic, but can't access the memories." He gazed at her for a moment. "Your connection allows you to sense and see them. It's quite remarkable."

"I still don't understand why." Ayleth frowned. "Does it have something to do with my birth parents?"

"Possibly."

"Shh. Stay still." Gabrian pointed to a thick copse of trees about fifty paces away. "It's there. Watch for movement."

Ayleth strained to see the deer among all the twigs and greenery. "I don't see it."

"Use your magic." He paused. "Sense it."

She closed her eyes, sent out a thin thread of magic, and searched. Within moments, a deer's fluttering breathing and nervous twitch brushed her fingertips. Excitement raced up Ayleth's arms and into her chest. She could feel its heartbeat. She opened her eyes. "What do I do?"

"Coax it into the open. Just like we practiced with the rabbits."

The sun glistened in the deer's eyes as it blinked and entered the meadow. It looked directly at them and twitched its ears.

"Now!" Gabrian said. "Do it now."

Ayleth raised her hands and gathered her magic. She took a deep breath to steady her quivering hands and sent a bolt of energy into the animal's heart. The deer groaned and dropped to the ground.

Gabrian and Ayleth raced to its side and knelt. It was still breathing.

"Quickly," Gabrian pushed Ayleth closer. "Search for its force and collect it."

The deer struggled to move as Ayleth focused on clasping its spirit. It took one last breath and stilled. Its glistening life essence flowed from its nostrils, hovered in the air for a moment, and disappeared.

Gabrian stepped to her side. "Did you snare it?"

She shook her head. "It escaped too quickly."

"Don't be discouraged," Gabrian said. "You've come a long way in a short time. It will happen soon."

He stood and motioned for the two guards to come forward. "Hang it up over there."

The men dragged the deer to a tree with a low overhanging branch, tied a rope around its hind legs, and hoisted it off the ground. "Do you want us to butcher it, sir?"

"No. Step back and let us finish." Gabrian pulled his dagger from his belt and handed it to Ayleth.

She took the heavy blade and stared at the still form before her. "It's much bigger than a rabbit. Where do I start?"

"Here," he pointed to a spot on the animal's abdomen. "Then cut up to here."

Ayleth sliced open the deer to expose the chest cavity and paused as steam from the warm organs gushed into the chilly air. Her hand dropped, and she looked away.

"Why did you stop?" Gabrian frowned. "Finish."

She carved deeper into the chest, cut out its heart, and handed it to Gabrian.

"You've completed a successful hunt." He nodded. "Finish the ritual."

Ayleth cut off a sliver, placed it into her mouth, and chewed slowly. She grimaced. The dead animal meant nothing to her. Its energy had escaped, and she had no desire to celebrate.

Gabrian nodded his approval and motioned for his men to come forward. "Bring it back to the keep. We'll have a feast tonight in Ayleth's honor."

They nodded and stepped toward the carcass with their knives drawn.

"Come." He stepped away from the men. "Our work is done."

Gabrian and Ayleth walked away.

The two guardsmen stared after them, their faces dark with disapproval.

Gabrian refilled Ayleth's mug with more watered wine and gestured at the uneaten food on her plate.

"Why so glum? It was a successful hunt."

She shoved her plate away and shifted in her seat.

"If you just needed meat for the table, you should have sent out your archers."

Gabrian cocked his head. "How can you expect to master your magic without practice? You're doing very well. When I was your age, I was still burning myself trying to start a fire."

She arched her eyebrow. "I doubt that."

He chuckled. "Well, not exactly, but it took a lot of trial and error."

Ayleth stared at Gabrian. "Where did your magic come from?"

"Just like you, from my father. He received his magic from his father, and so on, back to the beginning." Gabrian gazed out the window.

"It's not fair." She leaned her elbows on the table and rested her chin in her hands. "You know who your mother and father were. I don't."

Gabrian placed his hands on the table and leaned across.

"It doesn't matter. No one knows exactly why some people have magic and others don't. Leave those questions to the priests and monks. Focus on what's important."

"What's that?" She sat up and blinked.

His brow creased. "Your connection to dragons."

She crawled along the uneven ground toward a light glowing in the distance. The tunnel was dark, and sharp pebbles cut her hands and knees. As she scuttled closer, the sound of roaring fires and crackling stones grew louder. Where was she?

The intense light at the end of the tunnel made it hard to focus on the scene that opened up before her. A caustic smoke of sulfur and charcoal stung her nose. The intense heat forced her back into the tunnel. She wiped her eyes and cautiously moved towards the opening. Blinking tears away, she saw a massive cavern with a bubbling lake of molten lava filling its bottom. The liquid roiled and churned in orange fury. What is this place?

On the far side, a tiny figure, barely discernible, waved their arms and bellowed words that disappeared into the chaos. The lava pit rumbled louder and spat plumes of fire high into the air. Something moved within its depths, swirling toward the surface. A beast's head broke through and thrashed wildly. Wings sloshed out and beat, lifting an enormous body from the swirling liquid. Ayleth scrambled forward to the edge and looked on in disbelief—a dragon.

Ayleth woke with a cry, struggling to free her arms and legs from the bedsheets. She tumbled from the bed and moaned. Her skin was feverishly hot. She ran onto her balcony and slipped in the newly fallen snow. Tearing off her nightshirt, she scooped up handfuls of the icy slush and rubbed it against her blazing skin, seeking relief. She sank to her hands and knees and wept. Her tears sizzled as they dropped into the snow.

Bethyl scratched her chin and scowled. "What makes you think she's ready to become part of the Council?"

Gabrian glanced around the large, oblong table at the faces of his councilors. Bethyl's eyes narrowed, her face flushed. The two youngest counselors, Bronwyn and Theodoric, shifted nervously in their seats, and Burchard, his oldest advisor, looked up in alarm. Maryell, who had been with him almost as long as Bethyl, dropped her head forward and sighed. None of them offered their support. He didn't care. Ayleth had proven her magic could match theirs and even exceed them. It was time to include her.

"Are you questioning my judgment?"

"I am," Bethyl glared at him. "She's barely out of childhood, and her magic is still wild and uncontrolled. She should not be helping make decisions that will affect the future of Algowin."

"You're mistaken. Not only is Ayleth ready, but she is the future of Algowin."

Voices rose in clattering confusion as arguments spun around the table.

Burchard stood and raised his hand for silence. "I understand your desire to use her unique magic. But I share the others' concerns. She's young. It's unwise to rely on her without many more years of training."

Councilor Maryell tapped her fingers on the table. "You're letting your desire to reclaim the dragons cloud your judgment."

"What about the rest of you? Bronwyn? Theodoric?"

They looked down at their feet.

Gabrian scoffed. "I've made my decision. Now leave. All of you."

Everyone except for Bethyl shuffled out, grumbling and huffing. She stared across the table at him. "This is a mistake, Gabrian. You've stopped heeding the advice of your trusted advisors. When did you last seek me or anyone else out? It's madness."

Gabrian clenched his fists. "You're bitter because you turned your back on Ayleth, misjudging her magic."

Bethyl attempted to straighten her back and grimaced in pain, a constant reminder of Ayleth's attack. "That may be true, but you've fooled yourself into thinking you can control her. She will betray you once she realizes where her power comes from."

Gabrian waved at her. "Get out of my sight before I cripple you even more."

Ayleth touched the hem of the silk gown draped across her bed and frowned. Tonight, Gabrian was throwing a party. He hosted many over the years, but this evening was special. Ayleth was seventeen and no longer the solemn, mysterious child he had trained in secret. He wished to present her to his court as a young lady.

Her cat, Shadow, scurried from underneath the bed and brushed against Ayleth's legs. She picked him up and rubbed her face against the soft fur.

"You're lucky, Shadow. All you do is sleep and eat. No one controls your decisions and whereabouts all day.

The cat purred and crawled further onto Ayleth's shoulder. She pulled Shadow away and set her on the bed. "I wonder if I can sneak—"

The door creaked open, and Lenora's face appeared. "May I come in?" Ayleth nodded.

Lenora rushed over to the bed and gushed. "What a lovely dress."

"If you like it so much, why don't you wear it?" Ayleth scowled.

"Don't be cross. Gabrian picked it out, especially for tonight. You only get presented once, so you need to make it count." Lenora smiled at Ayleth.

"Presented sounds like you're leading a prize horse to market."

Lenora laughed. "It's not that bad. Only mages, staff, and a few nota-
bles from town will be present. He's not trying to marry you off."

"I'm not interested, so that's good." Ayleth crossed her arms.

"We need to get you ready. Go wash, including your hair, while I lay
out your jewelry."

Ayleth groaned and stomped around the corner into the bath.

Bethyl limped slowly down the corridor behind the dining hall into the
kitchen. She avoided the crowds and searched for a secluded spot to
witness the night's events unnoticed. Ever since Ayleth's outburst had
thrown her into a wall and broken her body, she was no longer Gabrian's
confidant and chief mage, relegated to minor tasks away from him and
Ayleth.

Climbing a narrow stairwell, she found a tiny alcove tucked high in
the back corner of the dining hall. Narrow slits in the wall allowed her
an overview of the entire floor, with its adorned tables overflowing with
the finest foods Algowin had to offer and the guests flowing in through
the main entrance. She sat on the hard stone bench for a long time and
dozed off.

Scraping benches and exclamations from multiple voices woke her.
She peered out as Gabrian entered the hallway with Ayleth on his arm.
She gasped. Ayleth was no longer the wide-eyed, skinny girl with wild
hair. At Gabrian's side was an elegant young lady in a flowing green silk
gown glistening with silver threads. Lenora had gathered Ayleth's white
braids and tucked them in place with an emerald-encrusted tiara that
sparkled in the candlelight. She nodded and greeted the assembled guests
with solemn grace.

Bethyl clutched her brooch. *How dare he present her in such a way?
The fool has thrown us all aside, and for what? A feral halfling!* Bile rose
in her throat, and she recoiled from the window. Gabrian's betrayal was
complete. She stood stiffly, shuffled back down the stairs, and began to
devise her plan.

CHAPTER FOUR

BETRAYED

The City of Sigor spread inland from a broad, protected harbor. Home to the king, it bustled with the comings and goings of an important port. The king's mages lived in the Imperium, just outside the castle walls near the town's orchards and gardens, where they practiced necromancy. Today, the place for the quiet study of magic buzzed with excitement. Rumors spread among the men and women who served inside these hallways — the king was planning to return dragons to Sigor.

"Has any of you ever seen a dragon?" a young female acolyte asked breathlessly.

Another student sitting beside her looked up from his book and rolled his eyes. "I see someone wasn't paying attention in history."

She narrowed her eyes and frowned.

"How could any of us see one? There've been no sightings in Sigor for centuries."

"I want to see one." She pouted. "Do you think the king will have us travel to Dragonswold? It would be so exciting."

Wilkin, the Imperium's librarian, peered over the top of his glasses and raised his eyebrows.

"Exciting? Will the Guardians of Dragonswold simply hand them over? If we go, some of you will die in the attempt."

The room quieted.

"You've trained to serve the king," Wilkin smirked. "You'll go wherever he orders you to go."

"Your Highness." The guard bowed low. "Algowin has sent a representative to see you."

King Eldridge straightened in his chair. "Algowin? Are you sure?"

"Yes." He extended a rolled parchment. "They asked me to give you this."

Eldridge accepted it and gestured for the messenger to wait as he opened it and read silently. The lines around the king's eyes deepened.

"Bring them to me."

The guard bowed and rushed out of the king's chambers.

Shortly, a young man in a heavy cloak entered and bowed. "Thank you for receiving me, Your Highness."

The king frowned. "Who are you?

"Stanhope, sir. I come at the request of one of the High Counselors of Algowin."

"Is this real?" The king waved the parchment. "What proof can you offer me that this young woman exists?"

Stanhope reached into the pocket of his surcoat and pulled out a dragon's tooth on a silver chain. He stepped forward and handed it to the king.

"This belongs to her. Perhaps you can identify her magic."

Eldridge clasped the chain tightly and brought it to his chest. The tooth pulsed with energy that was dark and foreign.

The king's eyes narrowed. "What are their terms?"

"They wish for sanctuary in the Imperium and your oath of protection from retaliation..." He paused.

"What else?"

"They request I return with enough coin to pay those who will assist." He bowed his head.

The king nodded. "Done. Bring the young woman to me."

Stanhope, Bethyl's apprentice, wrung his hands. "How do we remove Ayleth from here without Gabrian finding out?"

She scowled and shoved him back into a darkened alcove. "Let me worry about that. Just bring her to the forester's village. The King's Guard and a few mages will take us to Sigor."

"But..." he wrung his hands. "What if..."

"Stop worrying. She'll be out like a baby and won't be able to resist."

Stanhope shook his head. "I hope you're right. If she wakes up, I'm a dead man."

"Does this make you feel better?" Bethyl held out a leather pouch heavy with coins. "That should keep you comfortable once you get to Sigor."

He took it and bounced it in his palm, a crooked grin spreading across his face. "That seems fair."

"Good," Bethyl rubbed her hands together. "If everything goes as planned, there will be more once Ayleth arrives in Sigor. Get ready. I'll meet you at the stables."

He nodded and shuffled off around the corner.

Bethyl sighed and glanced up and down the dark and empty hall. "It's time."

The kitchen was empty except for one lone steward on duty, in case Lord Gabrian or any council members needed refreshments during the night. His eyelids fluttered, and his head drooped forward.

"You there?" Bethyl stepped into the kitchen.

He blinked, stood briskly, and straightened his back. "May I help you, Counselor?"

"Ayleth has requested her evening tea," Bethyl said. "I need you to take it to her."

He nodded and prepared a tray with a cup and saucer. He took a blue ceramic canister from a side shelf, carefully measured the tea, and placed it in a silver strainer. With great care, he poured hot water over the tea leaves into the cup.

"You've done this before, I see," Bethyl smiled sweetly.

The young man blushed.

"One more thing." Bethyl glanced toward the pantry. "Ayleth wants one of the honey cakes from this morning."

He vanished into the back room.

Bethyl took a pouch from her side pocket, dumped a silvery powder into the cup, and stirred.

Within moments, he emerged with a piece of cake on a small plate.

"Good lad," she said. "Now go quickly before the tea gets cold."

He picked up the tray and left.

She hurried back to her room, collected a large bag containing most of her belongings, and slipped into the hallway. She glanced both ways and hurried down the stairs and out the servant's entrance.

Ayleth moaned, rubbed her eyes, and stared at her blurry surroundings. She strained to sit up and fell back on the bed. A heavy metal bracelet rubbed against her skin. She frowned and tugged at the manacle, but it refused to budge. "What in Halia's…"

A disembodied voice greeted her. "Welcome to Sigor."

Ayleth blinked and stared at a hazy figure sitting in a chair several feet from the foot of the bed. "Where am I?"

"You're in the Imperium at Sigor. I'm Master Bregador, assistant to Archmage Rennick."

She shook her head to throw off the fog that enveloped her brain and sat up slowly. She shifted her legs over the side of the bed and stood. A length of chain clattered to the floor.

"Why have you imprisoned me?"

Bregador looked away, took a cloth from his pocket, and wiped his brow. "The Archmage requested it."

Ayleth glared at him. "Do you know I'm the assistant to the Lord of Algowin?"

He nodded. "Of course. That's why you're here."

She pulled against the chains. "These won't hold me."

Beads of sweat broke out on his brow.

She placed her palm on the manacle, which circled her left wrist and sent a bolt of magic into the metal. The clasp remained intact. She yanked frantically against the chain.

He stepped closer. "Stop. You'll hurt yourself."

She shot him an intense gaze. "What did you bastards do?"

"Quit struggling." He gazed at her. "Your magic is bound."

Ayleth hissed and bolted toward the door, pulling the bed with her.

Bregador threw his hands up. "Stop!"

She ignored him and yanked open the chamber door. "I'll see you in the fires of Othedon before I'll stay."

He yanked her into the room, stumbling against the bed.

Ayleth twisted under his arm to free herself.

He swung around and threw her to the floor.

"Would you prefer to be drugged constantly or listen to the king's offer?"

She snarled. "The king can mount donkeys."

Two guards rushed into the room.

Bregador motioned to them. "Come here and hold her down."

They knelt and clasped Ayleth's arms and legs.

"You've made your choice." Bredagor leaned over and pinched her chin tightly with his left hand. He forced her mouth open and dumped a vial of bitter liquid down her throat. "When you wake, maybe you'll reconsider."

Ayleth spat in his face and went limp.

Bregador shook Ayleth's shoulder roughly. "Get up."

She opened her eyes and blinked. He was close enough that she could smell his breath, which reeked of ale and fish. She glared at him and pushed herself up.

He took a step back.

"You're right to be afraid. As soon as I'm out of this," Ayleth rattled the restraint on her wrist, "I'll mount your head on a spire."

"I doubt that." He pulled his body taut to stop himself from trembling.

She surveyed the room. It was the same bedchamber, but the chain holding her captive was now securely anchored to the wall. She shifted forward until it was taut. There was just enough length for her to reach a washbasin, a small writing desk, and a chamber pot. She frowned. "What now?"

The Archmage will speak with you this morning. He walked to the door, opened it, and motioned for a woman with a tray to enter. She circled past him and placed the tray on a side table outside Ayleth's reach.

"What's your name?" Ayleth asked.

The woman looked at Bregador.

He nodded.

"Celestine, ma'am."

"You don't need to fear me. I know you had nothing to do with this," Ayleth held up her wrist. "Thank you for bringing my breakfast."

Nodding, Celestine exited the room.

"Sit back on the bed," Bregador ordered, "so I can place this closer."

Ayleth glared at him.

"As you wish." He placed the tray on the floor and shoved it toward her with his foot, spilling the tea and a small ceramic milk pitcher.

"I'll send Celestine back with some appropriate clothes for your meeting." He stomped out.

Ayleth struggled against the two guards, who clasped her arms firmly.

Bregador grimaced as he unlocked the wrist manacle. "They can drag you, or you can save your dignity and walk."

She quit struggling and followed them out of the room. They traversed a long hall lined with many doors and emerged into an outside courtyard. Ayleth mapped everything to memory and counted her steps, hoping she would remember later. They marched back inside, down another shorter hall, and stopped before a carved wooden door. Bregador grabbed a brass handle and pulled it open.

An older man in purple robes looked up from a table cluttered with manuscripts. He stood up to greet them. "Right on time. Good." He stared her up and down. "So, this is Gabrian's acolyte?"

"I'm right here," Ayleth huffed. "You can address me."

His eyebrows raised. "Are the mages at Algowin lacking manners?"

She hissed. "Not when they're kidnapped and imprisoned."

Gathering his robes, he moved regally across the room and stopped in front of Ayleth. He studied her for a few moments and placed his hand on her shoulder. "Why do you think you're here?"

She batted his arm away.

The guard directly behind her pinned her arms to her sides.

"You have no idea who or what you're dealing with. My name is Rennick, Archmage to the King. He requires your services. You'll treat me with respect, or I'll have you bound, gagged, and tied to your bed until we're ready to take what we need." He motioned for the guard to release her.

Ayleth rubbed her arms and twisted to face the door. She ducked past the guard and bolted across the room.

He raced after her and caught her as she yanked on the door handle. "Where are you going?"

She glanced over her shoulder. "Home."

"You ignorant woman." Rennick gasped and shook his head. "Algowin is not your home."

"Where then?" she hissed. "The floor of an old cabin, with a dirty blanket? That home?"

He smirked. "Gabrian bought you like a barnyard animal at auction. He doesn't deserve your loyalty."

"I don't give a donkey's ass what you think." She took several steps closer to the door.

Rennick raised his right hand and extended his index finger. His magic coiled around her like a whip and dragged her back into the room. "I'm not finished!"

Ayleth struggled to free her arms. "What do you want?"

He pulled her back into the room. "There are rumors you can call dragons. I need to see for myself."

She scowled. "Why should I help you?"

He tightened the magic binding and smirked. "Because if you don't, I'll harvest your magic for myself."

Ayleth paced across the room to the end of her chains and back to her bed. She must find a way to escape. She studied the pins in the rock wall, which were driven deeply and secured by magic. The manacles on her wrists simmered with spells as well. She sighed and collapsed on her bed.

The door creaked open, and a guard's head appeared.

"It's clear." He stepped back. "Go in."

Celestine appeared with a tray of food and a pitcher. She paused outside Ayleth's reach.

"I'll set this down by your bed if you promise not to hurt me."

"The worst I can do is wrestle you to the floor." Ayleth held up her shackled wrists. "What good would that do? Besides, I'm starving."

The young woman nodded and placed the tray on Ayleth's nightstand.

"It's not much, but it will keep you alive."

Ayleth grabbed a piece of bread, dunked it into the soup, and shoved it into her mouth. "Mm." She closed her eyes. "Thank you."

Celestine took several steps backward and turned to leave.

"Wait," Ayleth said.

Celestine hesitated. "Yes?"

Ayleth swallowed her mouthful. "Do you want to serve men who imprison women?"

Distress wrinkled Celestine's brow. "I don't understand what's happening. I..."

The door crashed open.

Bregador rushed in and pointed toward the door. "Out!"

Celestine gave Ayleth an apologetic glance and slipped into the hallway.

"She doesn't like what you're doing," Ayleth smirked.

Bregador stared at her. "She's young and doesn't understand."

Ayleth dunked another piece of bread into the soup. "Are you afraid I'll tell her?"

He pulled up a chair and sat. "Tell her what, exactly? That you and Lord Gabrian plan to use dark magic to enslave the dragons, and you'll destroy us all to do it?"

Ayleth sneered. "Are you going to pretend you won't destroy us for the same purpose?"

"None of this is necessary." Bredagor raised his chin and puffed out his chest. "The dragons rightfully fall under the king's command. It's the only way to ensure the kingdom's stability."

"It appears they're quite happy in Dragonswold." Ayleth eyed him. "They won't come willingly."

Bregador pursed his lips. "That's why we need your magic."

"You lost control of the dragons centuries ago. They were under the authority of Algowin before they fled to Dragonswold." Ayleth tilted her head. "You no longer have a claim to them other than your greed and lust for power."

He arched his eyebrow. "What about Lord Gabrian's lust for power?"

Ayleth stood, and the chain clanked to the floor. "I have nothing more to say. You're running out of time. Gabrian is probably already in the city looking for me."

"He may be, but dozens of mages hold a protective shield around the Imperium. He'll never get past it in time to save you." Bregador smirked.

She sat back on the bed and grinned. "Would you like to place a wager?"

Chapter Five

ESCAPE FROM SIGOR

Someone shook Ayleth's shoulder, and her eyes fluttered open. She moaned and attempted to stand, but her arms and ankles were bound to a heavy wooden chair. The room shifted as men and women in purple robes fanned out, encircling her.

"What are you donkey's asses up to?"

Archmage Rennick stepped forward and stood solemnly before her. He motioned to the others.

"We're going to release your magic and read its power."

"What?" Ayleth sat up straighter. Were they going to unbind her? She surveyed the room and counted heads. Fourteen. Ludager's balls. No chance, even for Gabrian.

Rennick nodded. "Let's see what you can do."

The mages clasped hands, and the room rumbled with their rhythmic chanting. Ayleth strained against the bindings as a dome of shimmering power appeared above her. The chanting intensified, and an oppressive heat pressed down on her skin. The burning increased until she cried out. A blinding light flashed inside the dome, and the pressure melted away as her magic poured out of her body, seeking escape.

She called the magic back into her hands and broke the bindings on her wrists. A quick flick toward her ankles freed her legs. She stood and rubbed her hands together. They sparkled with a familiar fire. Her magic was free.

Ayleth narrowed her eyes and glared at Rennick. She raised her hands and directed a searing bolt of magic directly at him. It bounced off the barrier and ricocheted inside the dome. She gathered her energy, more slowly this time, and pushed against the wall of magic. It bulged outward. She stepped forward and continued to press.

Unease flashed across Rennick's face. "Now!" The mages pulled the magic shield down onto Ayleth, collapsing her magic back into her body. The binding seared her skin as she crumpled.

Rennick wiped the sweat from his brow and cleared his throat. "Take her back to her room." Two guards stepped forward and dragged her away.

Bregador appeared at Rennick's side. "What do you think?"

"It was...she has..." Rennick cleared his throat. "She's more powerful than I thought."

Metal implements clanking into a bowl jarred Ayleth awake. Cold stone pressed against her back. She tried to move, but her hands and feet were bound. The smell of wet stone and mold assaulted her nose. She was somewhere dingy and damp. A rough wool blanket covered her body, but beneath it, a thin slip was the only thing protecting her from the chilled air and the stone at her back.

Rennick stepped into her view, holding a blade.

"What are you doing?" She struggled against the iron restraints.

He held the blade in front of her face. "I'm going to check your blood to see how much is human."

She thrashed sideways and kicked violently, tossing the blanket to the floor. The manacles tore into her flesh but did not budge. "Gabrian will kill you for this."

Rennick looked around the room. "Where is your liberator? We've neither seen nor heard from him. Perhaps he's not as powerful as you imagined."

She took several deep breaths and quit resisting, whispering a quick prayer that Gabrian would get there soon.

Rennick sliced her palm with a knife and collected her blood into a silver cup. She grimaced and looked away.

He returned the cup to a table filled with potions, powders, and bottles of dead things.

"Are you going to bind my wound?" Ayleth hissed.

Rennick motioned to a guard stationed at the door. "Clean that up and cover her."

The guard did as he was told.

Ayleth glared and pulled the blanket tighter. "I'll spend the rest of my time here deciding the best way to kill you. Slowly."

He turned and smirked. "By the time we drain your magic, you'll be a lifeless sack of skin and bones."

Her string of curses caused the guard to cringe.

Rennick mixed Ayleth's blood with an assortment of powders and tinctures. He twirled around so that she could see his face.

"To the truth." He drank the bloody brew. His hand shook, and he dropped the cup. His face contorted into a grimace. "By the gods," he sputtered.

Ayleth snickered. "I hope it kills you."

He tapped his chin. "Now it makes sense."

"What?" Ayleth frowned.

Rennick clasped his hands. "Your magic. It's searing, like the molten lava in the pits of Othedon."

"What are you saying?" Ayleth scoffed. "I'm the daughter of the Lord of the Underworld?"

His eyes widened. "Yes."

"You're crazy." She stared at him. "The gods aren't real."

He shook his head. "Every myth has its origin in truth. You've heard the tales of Xibor, Lord of the Underworld, haunting the kingdoms of men on the eve of a dark moon?"

"Yes, I know," she rolled her eyes. 'To seduce unsuspecting young women. They're nothing but scary stories to keep virgins from going out after dark."

"There have been tales of gods coupling with humans since the beginning." He leaned against the table. "Many of the lesser gods were believed to be half-human."

Ayleth snickered. "You think my mother slept with a god? Possibly a powerful mage, but not the Lord of Othedon. What a ridiculous fairytale."

"Not just any god, the one that created dragons." Rennick's chin quivered. "Gabrian kept you in the dark. He's known about your connection to Xibor's magic all along."

Was it true? Had Gabrian suspected and not told her? She scoffed. *Why should she believe anything Rennick says?*

"You don't need to believe me. The truth will be revealed soon enough." He gathered his things and strode toward the door.

"Sir," the guard said. "There's no chamber pot."

Rennick surveyed the room. "If she soils herself, throw a bucket of water over her."

The guard nodded and returned to his post by the door.

Ayleth woke from a restless sleep, shivering from the cold stone at her back. The room was dimly lit by a single candle in sconces on either side of the door. An unfamiliar guard stood rigid against the wall, his eyes staring across the room. Her palm was on fire from the knife cut, and her belly growled. She ignored the need to relieve herself to avoid the humiliation of being sloshed down with a bucket of cold water.

"What are you looking at?" The guard scowled.

"Nothing," Ayleth said. "What time of day is it?"

His chin quivered. "I'm not supposed to talk to you."

"It's going to get boring."

"No talking." He glared at her and looked away.

"What if I sing?"

"Be quiet, or I'll come over and shut you up."

She contemplated harassing him further, but he could do much worse than beat her up or bind her mouth. She took a deep breath and un-clenched her hands.

A knock on the door caught the guard's attention.

"State your purpose."

A low, raspy voice responded. "Food for the prisoner."

Ayleth's heart pounded with a flash of hope.

The door creaked open, and a man in a servant's robe entered, carrying a tray. He glanced over at Ayleth and nodded.

Her breath caught in her chest. *It's Gabrian! How can I distract the guard?* She inhaled and began to sing loudly. "Oh, the mighty warriors rode into the battle fray. It was their march to victory upon that fatal day."

The guard took a step forward. "Shut up, woman."

Ayleth ignored him. "They fought the enemy with swords held high and strong; the gods were on their side, they said, but dragons proved them wrong."

The guard leaned over and reached for Ayleth's throat.

Gabrian grabbed him by the neck and twisted. It snapped with a sickening crunch, and the man crumpled to the floor.

Ayleth gulped back a sob. "I was about to give up hope."

It took time to figure out how to enter without being noticed.

"Hurry." She closed her eyes. "I need to find a chamber pot."

Gabrian tapped the manacles, and they clicked open, clattering to the floor.

Ayleth sat up slowly and groaned.

"Let me help you." Gabrian clasped her arm and assisted her to stand. "There's a bucket over there."

She shuffled slowly into the corner.

Gabrian turned away.

Ayleth finished, found the blanket on the floor, and wrapped it around her body. "Bastards took my clothes."

"I see that. I wasn't able to bring anything, considering my disguise." He eyed the guard. "Take his clothes. They'll be big, but better than nothing."

She stripped the dead man of his coat, shirt, and breeches. The boots were too big, so she left them. She could run faster barefoot.

"Can you unbind my magic?" Ayleth turned to Gabrian. "I need it to fight if you expect to get out of here."

Gabrian frowned. "As soon as I do, every mage within these walls will sense it and be upon us. We need to sneak out. There are two guards outside, but I can take them easily."

Ayleth glanced at the door. "I don't know where we are, and mages are everywhere."

"I've been here for a few days scouting." Gabrian moved closer to the door. "There's a seldom-used hallway that leads out past the kitchen. We'll go for that."

"I don't like it." She pursed her lips. "If they discover us, I won't be of any help."

Gabrian closed his eyes and rubbed his forehead. "We're in an old, unused dungeon. We should be able to reach the main hallway without being discovered. Once we're down the corridor, I'll release your magic, and we'll make a run for it."

She nodded and pulled on the guard's baggy clothes.

The guards outside the door dropped to the floor, unconscious, the moment Gabrian entered the hallway. Ayleth and Gabrian stepped over their prone bodies and jogged down the dark passageway to a set of stairs. He held up his hand, and they stopped to listen. There were no sounds other than their labored breathing. They hurried up the stairs and put their ears to the door. The hallway was quiet.

"Listen carefully." Gabrian clasped her hand. "Take a left and go to the second door on the right. It goes out through a servant's entrance. If anything happens, keep going. I'll stay and engage anyone we encounter."

"But..." Ayleth's eyes opened wide.

"No arguments. You must get out," Gabrian set his jaw. "Follow the path to the orchard. I have men stationed there with horses. Don't wait for me. They'll lead you out of town."

She pursed her lips and nodded.

"Sit down and close your eyes," he said.

Ayleth sank onto the top step.

Gabrian put his hand on her head and whispered a spell.

She trembled, her head burning under his touch. Her magic built inside her chest, pushing against the binding. It burst violently from her palms in a blinding flash of light. She gasped for air and retched.

"Are you alright? Can you get up?" Gabrian asked.

She steadied herself against the wall and pulled herself to her feet. Energy pulsed through her veins, and her vision cleared.

"I'm fine. Let's go."

He cracked open the door and peeked into the corridor. It was empty. He motioned for Ayleth to come, and they bolted down the hallway. As they rushed past, they heard a scattered shuffling of feet and voices yelling in the side hallways. Turning right toward the servants' entrance, they ran into a young woman carrying a platter of food, knocking the tray to the floor.

Celestine gasped. "Ayleth?"

Ayleth raised her finger to her lips.

"I know her, Gabrian. She helped me."

"Go," Celestine whispered. "If anyone comes, I'll tell them you went the other way."

"Thank you." Ayleth clasped the young woman's arm.

Celestine nodded. "Go. Quickly!"

Ayleth and Gabrian raced down the hall and around a corner. A glowing bolt of magic flashed in their faces, shoving them to their knees.

Gabrian pushed Ayleth toward the door.

"Run and don't look back."

She flew down the steps and across the open lawn toward the trees. Several of Gabrian's guards stood just inside the orchard. They motioned her forward. She scrambled to them and bent over to catch her breath.

Gabrian backed out the door and down the steps, his palms facing toward his attackers. Two mages threw flashing bolts against his protective shield. He glanced over his shoulder to ensure Ayleth had made it to safety.

More mages appeared from around the side of the building and approached Gabrian, palms raised.

Ayleth stepped out of the shadows and waved her arms. "Over here, you whores!"

They skidded to a stop and turned toward her.

"Come on, you cowards, I'm right here." Ayleth danced about.

They exchanged glances and hesitated.

She gathered her magic and sent a fiery blast. They crumpled to the ground in a heap of ash.

Gabrian sprinted to her side.

"Get down!" He grabbed her and threw her to the ground.

Explosions rocked the building. Chunks of rubble and dust rained down around them.

Gabrian kept his protection spell around them, saving them from getting pummeled with debris.

Ayleth coughed. "You blew the place up? You should have warned me."

He snarled. "You disobeyed me."

"I saved you."

He shook his head. "Get up. We need to go. Except for the two you burnt to ash, we've only slowed them down."

The horses stomped nervously and snorted. Gabrian and Ayleth vaulted onto their backs and grabbed the reins.

She yanked her horse around in a circle to survey the damage.

A figure stumbled around the crumbled blocks at a corner of the building. It was Celestine. She wiped a bloody hand across her face.

Ayleth hesitated.

The guards struggled to keep the highly strung horse beneath him from bolting. "We must leave."

Celestine spotted Ayleth and motioned for her to go.

Ayleth glanced back again, nodded, and followed the mounted guards down the hill.

They burst onto the busy streets of Sigor. People milled around in confusion, some rushing toward the Imperium. They were too distracted to worry about a band of riders racing past.

Using magic to enhance the horse's energy, they rode swiftly back to Algowin, with only an occasional break for rest and food. Ayleth strained to stay on her horse, so she tied herself to her saddle.

It was late evening when the towers of the keep, blazing with torches, appeared above the treetops. Gabrian urged his horse forward until he rode next to Ayleth.

"Hang on. We're almost there."

Her eyes cracked open, and she nodded. "Was it Bethyl?"

Gabrian nodded. "She and her apprentice disappeared at the same time you did."

Ayleth grimaced. "At some point, I'll find her and mount her head on a pike."

"She's probably hiding out in Sigor." Gabrian stared into the night. "I'll send some men to check around."

"Good. Have her brought to me alive so she can die slowly." Ayleth sneered.

Gabrian nodded.

Cassian and the night guard greeted them as they rode into the courtyard.

"I don't believe any soldiers followed us," Gabrian said. "But just in case, send a scout and put extra guards on the walls."

"Yes, sir," Cassian nodded and shouted orders to his men.

Gabrian slid off his horse and helped Ayleth to the ground. They linked arms and limped up the steps and into the keep.

Chapter Six
DRAGON'S CALL

Ayleth wound her way through Gabrian's cluttered study toward the open balcony door. Cold gusts of air brushed her face. It had been a month since their escape from Sigor, and she had seen little of him. This morning, he sent word that he wanted to speak with her.

Gabrian stood at the banister, staring into the deep canyon that dropped steeply below. A table to his left held his dragon's skull.

She cleared her throat.

Gabrian turned and motioned to the table. "There's something I need you to do."

"What?" Ayleth blinked.

He studied her. "You know how to connect with dragon memories in their bones."

"And..." She tilted her head.

He took a deep breath. "I want you to call one to us."

Her jaw dropped, and she stepped back.

Gabrian clasped his hands. "The king planned to use your magic to bring the dragons back to Sigor. Now that he's lost that option, he'll come to take them by force. We must warn the dragons and negotiate an alliance."

Ayleth blinked again. "You believe I have some magical ability to talk with dragons?"

"Possibly," he half-smiled.

She folded her arms across her chest. "Why? What do you know about my parents?"

Gabrian frowned. "What is this about?"

"Do you know what Archmage Rennick told me?"

Gabrian stared at her. "No. How could I?"

She narrowed her eyes. "He said you knew all along about my connection to Xibor and the lava pits of Othedon."

Gabrian's eyes shifted. "I had my suspicions, but I've never been one to take stock of the gods or their stories, and neither have you."

"My mother was so afraid of me she left me to die. The other people who kept me from being eaten by wolves sold me to you. That is not a normal childhood." She crossed her arms. "You knew something, or you would never have come for me."

He pursed his lips. "Stories about a strange child in the forest were circulating in Sigor. I didn't know what it meant until I held you."

She glared. "Didn't know what?"

"That you had unnatural magic." He sighed. "There was no way for me to be certain how or from whom."

She considered him for a moment. "But you had an idea?"

"I wasn't sure of anything, not until you saw images when you touched the dragon's skull." Gabrian stared toward the mountains. "Until then, I never fully believed the gods were real."

Ayleth closed her eyes. *What could she remember? Certainly not her mother. The woman abandoned her soon after birth. Her first memory was toddling off into the forest, following a bobbing light. Her adoptive mother had chased after her and warned her about running after fairy lanterns. She continued to sneak into the forest to look for things that glowed, finding stones, animal bones, and rocks that all shed an unnatural light as if calling to her. She never felt afraid or alone. Someone or something was watching over her. Then the bones spoke to her. Not in words but in feelings: the warmth of a cozy burrow, the joy of soaring through treetops, the tenderness of a soft nuzzle. Because she had always sensed them, it seemed natural.*

She opened her eyes and placed her fingertips on the animal skull in her pocket, the first one that had ever spoken to her. She gazed at Gabrian. "Why me?"

"It doesn't matter how you came by your magic," Gabrian drummed his fingers on the banister. "It's only important that you possess it."

"For what purpose?"

Gabrian placed his hand on Ayleth's shoulder. "I worship no gods and spend little time worrying about their existence. Still, whether we believe in them or not, their hand is in this."

"What if I don't want it?"

"I don't believe that." He placed a finger under her chin and lifted her face to his. "You and I can bring the dragons back to Algowin. It's what we both want."

Ayleth walked around him to the balcony's edge and stared into the sky. *Could they do it?* The thought made the magic in her blood flare. *Gabrian was right. She wanted this as much as he did.*

"What do you need me to do?"

"Place your hands on the skull and focus on whatever magic you can sense. Once you connect, reach out and scan for any dragon energy close by."

She nodded and placed her hands on top of the skull. Sparks of energy crackled around her fingers. She closed her eyes and released her magic. A spinning warmth traveled up her arms. Images of a dragon torn from the sky by a poisoned arrow appeared in her mind. It struggled on the ground, breathing fire and lashing out against the armed warriors that closed in on all sides. The skull under her fingertips belonged to a dragon killed in battle. It had fought valiantly until the end.

The image faded and Ayleth opened her eyes. She gazed up at the peak of a mountain far to the east.

A dragon hovered, gazing in her direction.

Her heart beat wildly with excitement. *Had it heard her?* She reached out with her thoughts. *Come to me.*

It arched its head back and waited.

She tried again. *Come to me.*

The giant silver-grey dragon glided for several minutes down the mountain slopes before hovering in front of the balcony. It peered at them intently.

Ayleth gasped. All the images of dragons she had seen in Gabrian's books and on his walls didn't compare with the magnificence of a real one. It was beyond anything she could have imagined.

Its voice roared in her head. [What do you want?]

"I'm Ayleth. This is Gabrian, Lord of Algowin. I summoned you."

[I'm Jiormason. No one summons me. I came to see who has the magic to speak to me.]

Ayleth clutched her chest and stared.

The dragon shook his head impatiently. [What is it?]

She swallowed deeply. "You're in danger."

[From whom?] Jiormason tilted his head.

Ayleth turned to Gabrian. "What should I tell him?"

"The King of Sigor plans to send troops to destroy the Guardians and force the dragons to serve under his command." Gabrian glanced from Ayleth to the dragon.

She relayed his message.

A deep rumble rolled from the dragon's belly. [He may try, but he will fail.]

She turned to Gabrian and repeated the dragon's words.

Gabrian continued. "Tell him if they don't comply, the king will destroy Dragonswold and the Guardians."

Ayleth told Jiormason of their impending doom.

The dragon looked perplexed. [Why are you telling me this?]

"Because we can help you stop them." Ayleth took a deep breath.

Jiormason eyed her. [At what price?]

She stared at the dragon. [Your return to Algowin.]

The dragon's nostrils flared, and smoke poured out.

[So, we are to trade one overlord for another?]

Gabrian cleared his throat, and Ayleth told him what the dragon had said.

"Tell him we would be..." Gabrian spread his palms wide, "...allies."

She shared Gabrian's words.

The dragon shook his head. [You take us for fools. We remember our history. The ancient mages of Algowin enslaved us. We were not allies.]

Ayleth glared at Gabrian. "They were your slaves?"

Jiormason snarled. [Do not bother me again.]

Ayleth slammed her fist onto Gabrian's table. "Why didn't you tell me?"

He cleared his throat. "I was waiting for the right time."

"Donkey's ass." She glared at him. "Algowin enslaved the dragons, and you kept it from me?"

He sputtered. "You weren't ready."

"Really?" she arched her eyebrow. "Were you afraid I'd not trust you?"

He threw up his hands. "I hoped it wouldn't be necessary this time."

She picked up a book and tossed it to the floor. "Ludager's balls, Gabrian. Is reclaiming their magic worth it?"

"You just spoke with one. What do you think?"

Ayleth glared at him and stormed out onto the balcony. She wrapped her arms around the dragon's skull and struggled to pick it up.

Gabrian rushed out after her. "What are you doing?"

She narrowed her eyes. "I'm taking it to my study. It's mine now."

He stepped aside and let her pass.

"Think about the magic. We must protect it."

Books tumbled to the floor as Ayleth shoved the skull onto the table. Her head buzzed from contact with the bone. She shuddered and brushed the energy from her arms. She needed time to think. Sigor would attempt to capture the dragons by force, and Jiormason had sworn to resist to the death. There must be a way to convince the dragons to join Algowin so their magic wouldn't disappear.

Her mouth went dry at the thought of them being slaughtered. She poured herself a mug of water and gulped it down. It was no longer solely about Gabrian's desire to control the dragons but about their existence. She picked up her books from the floor, returned them to their proper shelves, and cleared the table of everything except the skull and a few candles. She removed the small animal skull she'd kept from her childhood in her pocket and placed it next to the larger one. Bones had spoken to her before, and maybe they held the answer. It was time to claim her connection to dragon magic.

Gabrian never summoned Ayleth to his private chambers. Tonight, however, he invited her to dine with him there. She was puzzled by the change in him since their encounter with the dragon. He was more patient with her in her studies. Instead of criticizing her lack of knowledge, he complimented her progress, touching her shoulder in encouragement when pointing out important passages in whatever journal they were studying. He had shown no affection or pride previously. It was unsettling.

What did he wish to discuss in private? Was he angry with her? She had kept up with his grueling study schedule and agreed to summon a dragon. She had forgiven him for not telling her about the dragon's bondage. There was no time left to consider his motives. While lost in thought, the afternoon sped away. Ayleth pulled her hair back into a ponytail and threw on a simple high-waisted shift instead of the more formal wear required in the dining hall. It was time to go.

Gabrian's door stood cracked open, and she heard voices within. As she approached, several young women from the kitchen staff emerged, carrying empty trays. They bowed to her and hurried down the hallway. She peeked around the door. A formal table sat before the fireplace with candles and crystal goblets. The table overflowed with multiple platters of meat, vegetables, loaves of bread, and sweet delicacies. She paused and cleared her throat.

Gabrian looked up and motioned for her to enter. "Please come and sit." He poured her a cup of red wine.

"What are we celebrating?" Ayleth asked.

"You. Us. The future," Gabrian smiled at her.

She leaned forward. "Aren't you getting ahead of yourself? We have to win control of some dragons first."

He picked up his goblet. "We do, and that's just the beginning," he said, handing her the other. He raised his glass in tribute. "To you, Ayleth. Thank you for saving my life."

She clasped the crystal cup and clinked it against his. "You're welcome."

He placed his goblet on the table and shifted around to pull out her chair.

She stepped forward, a puzzled look on her face.

"You're making me nervous. Are you preparing to ask me to ride a dragon or sneak into Dragonswold and steal their eggs?"

Gabrian chuckled. "If I thought you'd be successful, I might."

Ayleth scoffed. "We have enough problems without inviting an all-out war."

"We may not have a choice, but I want to discuss what comes after that." Gabrian studied her.

She leaned back in her chair and folded her arms. "Are we going to talk or eat?"

"We can do both." He motioned toward the dishes. "Please, help yourself."

She rolled her eyes and served small helpings from each platter. The dessert was pomegranate tarts. She smiled. Gabrian knew these were her favorites.

They ate in silence for a few moments.

Ayleth took a sip from her goblet. "What about it? If we don't all die, we'll have dragons and power. What else is there?"

"Exactly that." He tilted his head. "We will be in control of everything. People will look to us to lead."

"What do you mean by 'us'?" She frowned. "You're a lord. Go get yourself a lady."

"I've never found the right person; hence, I have no heirs." He smiled sadly.

Ayleth stared at him. "Stop. If you say I'm like a daughter, I'll throw my wine glass at you."

He coughed. "I know you don't see me as family, but I'd like you to consider being next in line to rule at Algowin if something should happen to me."

Ayleth considered his unexpected offer. Gabrian's plans were always controlled and deliberate, so what was his game? *Can I trust him to share his power, let alone pass it on to me?* She would keep her doubts to herself and wait.

CHAPTER SEVEN

BATTLE OF DRAGONSWOLD

A horse clattered into the courtyard, its sides lathered in sweat. The rider dismounted and sprinted up the stairs and into the foyer. "I have news for Lord Gabrian." He waved a leather messenger pouch above his head.

Cassian hurried in behind him, his hand on the hilt of his sword. "Declare yourself."

The man swiveled around. "Darian, sir. I have news about King Eldridge."

"Give me the message." Cassian extended his hand.

"With all due respect," Darian backed away. "I will only give it to the Lord of Algowin."

"Very well," Cassian said. "Follow me."

They hurried up the stairs to Gabrian's study. Cassian pounded on the door.

"Enter," Gabrian said.

Cassian stepped into the room and motioned for Darian to follow. "My lord, a rider here from Sigor."

Gabrian took the packet, pulled out the message, and read it silently. His brow furrowed.

"King Eldridge is moving his regiments toward Dragonswold." Gabrian turned to Darian. "How many days ago?"

"Two or three, my lord. I rode here when I saw the men assembling at the garrison."

"Thank you for getting here so quickly." Gabrian clasped Darian's shoulder. "Cassian, get him fed and stable his horse, then call the council to their chambers."

Cassian put his fist on his heart, bowed, and escorted Darian out of the room.

Gabrian brushed open the large parchment map with the palm of his hand and anchored down the corners with several polished stones. "Here." He pointed to a spot on the map. King Eldridge will lead his army to engage near the mountains, before the boundary of Dragonswold.

Arguments erupted among the council members.

"Quiet." Gabrian gazed around the room. "It's the only thing that makes sense. Guardians are expert archers used to fighting in dense forests. If the king's soldiers wanted to flush them out, they would have to separate into small groups, making themselves easy targets. King Eldridge must draw the Guardians out into the open and hope the dragons will follow."

Cassian cleared his throat. "What will we be doing?"

Gabrian cleared his throat. "Nothing."

The room buzzed with alarm and dissension.

Gabrian held up his hand. "Let the king's troops and the Guardians exhaust themselves in combat before we intervene."

Several voices muttered their approval.

Ayleth studied the map. "Where will we be?"

"There's a spot on the mountain just west of the Dragonswold border." Gabrian placed a small stone on the map. "A series of switchbacks leads up to a broad ledge. We'll be able to see the battle undetected."

She rubbed her chin. "When will I speak with the dragons?"

Heads swung sharply in her direction.

Burchard, Gabrian's senior advisor, glanced from Ayleth to Gabrian. "What's she talking about? You can't seriously think this young woman has that type of power?"

"She does." Gabrian grinned. "She's already summoned one."

The room erupted into chaos.

Ayleth stood on the high ledge overlooking the broad, open grasslands with Gabrian and his five counselors. They lined up in front of a low table that held his dragon skull, staring at the valley below.

Row after row of soldiers moved steadily across the open grasslands toward the base of the mountains.

"How many are there?" Ayleth shaded her eyes from the glaring sun.

"It's less than a legion, fewer than I expected, but look." Gabrian pointed to the rear of the advancing troops. "See the wagons surrounded by the king's guard? He's brought all his mages with him. They'll strengthen their soldiers and weapons with magic."

Ayleth clenched her fists. "We can't just stay here and watch. We need to…"

Gabrian held up his hand and motioned toward the valley.

A guardian with long, grey hair tied back with a strip of leather emerged from the trees. He wore a simple brown cape and carried a sparkling scepter in his left hand. Moving forward, he halted just outside of arrow range.

The king's army came to a halt. Horses stomped impatiently as riders shifted in their saddles.

King Eldridge wore full battle armor and rode through the columns on his white stallion. His captain rode behind him, carrying the banner of Sigor. They stopped when they reached the front of the ranks. The king dismounted, handed the reins to his captain, and strode forward until he stood fifty paces from the guardian.

The Guardian stared at the king. "You're a long way from home."

Eldridge smirked. "You know why I'm here, Vynrith. Will you stand aside, or do you wish to die with the rest of the Guardians?"

Vynrith shifted the wand to his right hand. "The dragons wish to remain in Dragonswold. Why fight a battle you can't win?"

The king turned and waved toward his troops. "As you can see, we're ready to destroy you and your magic."

Vynrith eyed him. "What about the dragons? Will you kill them, too?"

"They know the choice: come with us willingly, or we will crush Dragonswold." The king smirked.

Vynrith sighed. "Very well." He raised both arms into the air and chanted. The ridges of the surrounding mountains moved as dragons perched on rocky crags took to the sky. Soon, the horizon behind Vynrith was full of hovering dragons awaiting his command.

The king shook his head. "You're a fool, old man. We'll kill you and your men, then bind the dragons to me." He turned and sprinted to his horse, vaulting into the saddle. He raised his sword above his head and shouted above the sounds of shifting armor and rattling spears. "To Dragonswold!"

Ayleth's heart jumped when Jiormason emerged from over the mountain and flew to the front of the dragons gathered for battle. She clenched her fists as magic threatened to leap from her palms. *It's happening. They're here, and they're magnificent. What if Gabrian is right? Can we bring them back to Algowin?* She debated whether to contact Jiormason and inform him of their presence. Not wanting to distract him in the midst of battle, she waited.

Vynrith lowered his arms, and Jiormason dropped from the sky to soar over the front ranks of the soldiers, spraying them with fire. It bounced off the protective shield held in place by the king's mages. The king's foot soldiers surged forward, followed by archers on horseback. Behind them, sturdy carts rolled on with massive crossbows designed to shoot heavy lances. The wagons bearing the king's mages took up the rear. When they reached the mountain base, Guardians surged from between the trees, racing forward with their swords raised. Their weapons pommeled the shimmering spell of protection with loud clangs and sparks. Dragon magic embedded in their blades created weak spots in the enchanted shield, and they slipped through to engage the king's warriors.

Dragons raced from overhead, concentrating their fire on the wagon full of mages. The shield above the king's troop faded as the alarmed necromancers pulled their magic tighter to protect themselves.

Ayleth gasped as sunlight sparkled on the point of a lance that raced upward to pierce through the neck of a dragon.

Gabrian grimaced and shook his fist. "What is that fool of a king doing?"

Ayleth grabbed Gabrian's sleeve. "He's killing them."

"He knows," Gabrian groaned.

"Knows what?" Ayleth stared at him.

"That we plan to step in and take control; the bastard will kill them all before he lets that happen." He punched the air with a fist.

Her hand tightened on his arm. "I'm not waiting. I'm going down."

"No!" Gabrian clasped Ayleth's shoulders. "Listen closely. Reach out to Jiormason. Tell him we'll help. He needs to relinquish control to you."

She placed her hand on the skull and took a deep breath. *Jiormason. Can you hear me?*

Gabrian surveyed the sky for a glimpse of the silver-grey dragon and pointed. "He's there."

Ayleth closed her eyes and concentrated more deeply. *Jiormason, we'll help you destroy the king's army. Send your magic to me.*

The dragon paused high above the battlefield and turned her way. [We will not relinquish our magic or our freedom—not to you, not to anyone.]

Please, Jiormason. The king won't stop until you're all dead.

[Then we will rest at peace with our ancestors.]

Gabrian shook her arm. "What's he saying?"

She opened her eyes and stared at the dragon hovering in the distance. "He said they would rather die than give up their freedom."

Gabrian turned and motioned for his councilors to gather at his side.

"We must destroy the spell protecting the king's soldiers."

They gathered in a circle and held hands. Gabrian chanted. A spiral of energy rose above their heads and sped off like a tornado toward the wagon, sheltering the king's mages. The glistening shield of magic shattered into flying sparks of energy, and the mages scattered into the trees at the forest's edge.

Dragons swooped from the sky to attack the exposed soldiers. The air was heavy with arrows and lances. Ayleth watched in horror as several dragons dropped from the sky. *What had they done?*

The dragons were determined to destroy the king's army, even as their ranks dwindled. If they did not win, the king would return with a larger army and try again. Jiormason urged them on. Ayleth's pleas buzzed around his head. He resisted. For centuries, the dragons had known complete freedom allied with the Guardians. He would never surrender his authority to the King of Sigor or the Lord of Algowin.

The battle continued for hours, one side gaining advantage, then the other. The Guardians hacked their way through the protective shield, only to be driven back by a fresh surge of magic. Many soldiers had fallen to the Guardian's magical blades, but the bodies of the Dragonswold defenders littered the battlefield as well.

On the ledge high above the battleground, Gabrian and his counselors pulled their magic together and directed it against the king's mages. Ayleth cast spells to protect the dragons, and they all grew exhausted from the effort.

Gabrian dropped his hands and let the flow of magic collapse onto the ground.

"Why did you stop?" Ayleth asked.

He gestured towards a rocky outcrop across the field. "The king's mages are gathered behind that big jumble of boulders. They outnumber us, and we don't have enough magic to stop them. We must pull the dragons out of this battle."

Ayleth glanced from the skull to the dragons, soaring through rising smoke and flying arrows. "If I can amplify my magic using the skull, it's possible I can bind them to me." She hurried to the skull, placed her hands on top, and repeated words from the spell to gather their magic. Gabrian and his council gathered around her and joined their voices to hers.

A magic thread pulsed up from the rocks below, coiled up Ayleth's legs, and collected in her chest. When she could no longer contain it, it surged down her arms into the skull, which glowed with an unearthly light.

"Good," Gabrian nodded. "Connect with Jiormason's spirit."

She narrowed her focus to the dragon hovering in the distance.

Jiormason momentarily lost control of his wings and struggled to stay in flight.

Her mind connected to his anger and alarm. She pulled tighter and held on.

The dragon jerked and severed the connection, sending Ayleth, Gabrian, and the councilors flying into the air and landing on the rocky ground.

A silent horror filled Jiormason's chest as he hovered over the smoky battlefield. Slowly turning in a circle, he searched the sky to see who remained. A handful of dragons continued to swoop down on the troops and clash against the magic that protected them. A light flashed from an outcropping of massive boulders at the far edge of the battlefield. He flew closer and spotted men in purple robes clustered amongst the rocks—the king's mages.

Jiormason prayed to the ancestors, tucked his wings against his sides, and dropped like a bird of prey chasing a rabbit. He crashed headlong into their hiding place, crushing rocks and bodies. The protection spell evaporated, and the soldiers began to fall under the dragon's fire. Those who remained turned to flee. The king rode his horse back and forth against the retreating men, ordering them to stand their ground. Some obeyed, and others continued their panicked retreat.

Gabrian and Ayleth watched as the final two dragons fell from the sky, victims of the deadly lances.

Gabrian turned to Ayleth. "You need to go down."

"And do what? We've failed." She pointed at the smoldering battle-field. "They're all dead."

Gabrian closed his eyes and placed his hands at his temples. "Not all. Don't you feel it?"

Hope rose in Ayleth's chest. Maybe Jiormason was still alive.

She stumbled to the dragon skull that lay shattered on the rocky ground. She picked up a tooth and clutched it tightly, closing her eyes to concentrate. There was a heartbeat, weak but steady. It had a familiar rhythm, but it was not Jiormason.

Chapter Eight
From the Ashes

E mbers from burning grass floated across the battlefield, flickering and dying in the encroaching twilight. Ayleth leaned heavily on a broken spear shaft and peered through the shifting grey smoke. It was becoming harder to distinguish between the dark shapes on the ground. Were they man, horse, or dragon? She searched for signs of life, seeking any movement in the shadows. On top of a rise in the distance, a shadow shifted. A massive figure scraped against the rocky soil, falling heavily back onto the ground. Her heart leaped despite her exhaustion. The dragon was still alive. She forced her weary legs to ascend quickly. She had to hurry. There was little time.

Struggling to shift her large frame upright, the wounded dragon could not stand. The lance that pierced Emelthedin's chest and protruded from the top corner of her wing made every breath agony. The weapon was poisoned or enchanted, so her time was short. Drifting tendrils of smoke and the approaching darkness limited her vision. Straining to find signs of other living beings, she heard only the distant cries of wounded humans and crackling fires. The air hung thick with smoke and death. Had any of her clan survived the slaughter?

There was no fire left in her rasping lungs, so she raised her head for an anguished roar. Today, her entire family had perished. She watched her father, Jiormason, fly high above the clouds and turn to dive into the rocks that sheltered the king's mages. She had turned away, unable to bear the sight of him crashing to his death. The fighting stopped momentarily, but it was little comfort. Her beloved father lay crumpled and unmoving at the base of the mountain.

Dasmarg, her brother, fell defending the Guardians from the oncoming army of soldiers, protected by magic. From their eldest to youngest, dragons bravely charged their enemies, dodging enchanted spears. They descended through the hail of arrows toward the approaching battalion, clawing and breathing fire to burn them away.

What means of dark magic had defeated the combined forces of dragons, the Guardian mages, and the defenders of Dragonswold that fought at their side? She had no answer. Even if she had known, what could she have done to save them? She prayed in memory of the fallen and begged whatever gods were listening to bring Vynrith, the Guardian's Dragonkeeper, to this bloody battlefield so he could release their spirits to the ancestors.

As darkness fell, she lost faith. Was the Dragonkeeper still alive? What would happen to her soul if he had perished? Who would chant the sacred words to release her spirit to the ancestors? Were any dragons still alive to stand with Vynrith and breathe fire to burn her bones to ash? She despaired at the thought of being kept captive here for eternity, her essence trapped as her bones bleached in the sun. She stilled her mind and pushed her awareness out, searching for any life around her. A heartbeat approached. She was not alone. Perhaps there was still hope.

She blinked ash from her eyes and strained to see movement amongst the shadows. Something trudged uphill from the battlefield. Was it a man or a beast? A figure emerged from the smoke: a tall female mage with pure white hair, dressed in a ragged and stained robe. The woman stopped and stared at the dragon, exhaustion creasing her face.

Emelthedin huffed a tiny stream of fire and smoke in disgust. She recognized the robe and the telltale brooch pinned to the woman's collar. She served Gabrian, the Lord of Algowin—the godless mage who stood by and watched Emelthedin's family slaughtered by the king's army.

[Who are you? What do you want?] Emelthedin snarled.

The woman stumbled closer to Emelthedin. "I'm Ayleth from Algo-win. Lord Gabrian sent me to find you. I'm here to help."

[Why?]

"I cannot permit all of you to die. Let me see what I can do." Ayleth's fingers followed the shaft to where it entered the dragon's body. She could not remove it; the lance was embedded too deeply. She trembled. The dragon was going to die.

Ayleth moaned in frustration. "Why didn't Jiormason listen to me?"

[Stupid child. You'll never understand what it means to be a dragon, to have the freedom of the sky, and to live life on your terms.]

"I think I might." Ayleth frowned as she stared at the spear's shaft.

The dragon's head collapsed, and her eyes fluttered before closing. She was still breathing, but just barely.

Ayleth dropped to her knees at the dragon's head. "What's your name?"

[Emelthedin.]

"Jiormason could have stopped it. This is his fault."

[Says the one who would enslave us.]

Emelthedin took a deep breath, her nostrils flaring. [You have dragon magic. I can smell it. You've betrayed your own blood.]

Ayleth clasped her chest. "I never wanted this."

[Then help me. Burn me and release my soul.]

"I can't permit you to die and take your magic with you."

The dragon snarled. [Then curse you to the fires of Othedon.]

A deep, rasping breath rattled in Emelthedin's chest, and she slid into unconsciousness.

Ayleth yanked implements from a leather pouch: a metal pot, a sharp knife with a curved blade, bags of powder, and tiny pieces of bone. The gathered ingredients were set on the ground next to the pot. She emptied water from her skein and threw in the powders, followed by the bone fragments. She reviewed her preparations before starting a fire and balancing the pot on the hot coals.

Moving to Emelthedin's side, Ayleth placed her hand on the dragon's chest. She was alive, but not for much longer. Ayleth stumbled to the fire to prepare for the ritual Gabrian had insisted she learn—a binding spell to capture the souls of animals. She had started small, with birds and squirrels, and then with larger prey, like wild boar and elk. It had drained her magic to the point of unconsciousness and succeeded with only the smaller creatures. Now she understood what he was training her to do. She shook her head. He must have known it might come to this.

She clasped the dagger in her hand. Bile rose in her throat as she realized what she needed to do. She doubled over and vomited until nothing was left but dry heaves. A spiral of dark magic rose from the stone beneath her, and her veins burned; it wound around her and grew until she glowed white hot. Her ears roared with the sound of crackling fire and bubbling cauldrons. A vision from her dream of the god-demon standing by a molten pool of lava filled her head. His image stared at her and raised his hand. *Dragon magic is your birthright. Claim it.*

She stood trembling and turned to face Emelthedin. *Jiormason was wrong. We could have been allies. Forgive me. I cannot let dragon magic die.*

Ayleth gritted her teeth and plunged the knife into Elmelthedin's throat. She filled a silver cup with the blood that poured from the wound and brought it back to her fire. The energy coursing through her veins guided her movements as she poured the dragon's blood into the pot. *What if the dragon's blood is not enough?* There was no time for doubt or hesitation. "Rosthar, sune elasthar," she chanted loudly and slashed her wrist, letting her blood pool with Emelthedin's. She fought to stay conscious as the rich reds sizzled and swirled, combining with the powdered potions. Gone was any pain or fear. Her only thought was to capture the dragon's spirit. As her vision narrowed to a tiny pinprick of light, she picked up the bowl and drank deeply. The roaring essence of a dragon swirled around her as she collapsed onto her side, spilling the remaining liquid into the dirt. Her bloody fingers clawed at her chest, which burned with Elmelthedin's rage.

CHAPTER NINE
FINAL JOURNEY

A deathly silence met the night as it descended over the battlefield. The ravens and vultures had left their feast to return at first light. Gabrian stumbled across the uneven ground, searching for Ayleth. His floating mage lanterns were of little help against the dark as his magic searched for anything alive. It guided him toward men and animals in their last moments of life. But none of them were her.

A whisper of magic brushed his brow. He stopped to listen. The thread of faint energy pointed him to someone or something that still breathed. He hurried toward the source. The lanterns illuminated a dragon, its lifeblood spilled on the ground, and a figure lying on its side next to it. He rushed over and knelt. It was Ayleth.

He touched her brow.

"Ayleth. Can you hear me?"

She did not respond. Gabrian tried to roll her onto her back, but a stiff bundle of folded leather held her in place. He drew his lantern closer, and the blood drained from his face—wings emerged from her back. He brushed wisps of hair away from her forehead and traced a finger along the scales sparkling at her temple. His breath quickened. *Ayleth didn't absorb the dragon's magic; she merged with it. How is this possible?*

Gabrian stood, took off his cloak, and spread it out. Scooping his arms underneath Ayleth, he carefully lifted her onto the cloth and wrapped it snugly around her. He searched for her thoughts, but they hid behind a shield of darkness. She was not dead, but she was not alive either. He had read about people turned into half-beasts by sorcerers' enchantments, but always dismissed them as fairy tales. The locals would consider her a demon. His counselors would believe her a monster created with tainted magic. He tried repeatedly, but none of his healing spells could wake her. His only option was to take her back and tell them she was dead until he figured out what to do.

Before he left, there was one last ritual he needed to perform to honor the dragon's sacrifice. Gabrian and Ayleth always did it at the end of each hunt. He stumbled over to the body of the slain dragon, slipping in the blood-slicked mud. Sliding a dagger from its sheath, he plunged it into the dragon's chest and cut out its heart.

Cassian was waiting for Gabrian at the front gate. His face paled when he spotted the tightly bound bundle secured to the horse's saddle and Gabrian's blood-stained tunic. He rushed forward. "What happened? Is she alive?"

"No. I'm afraid she's gone." Gabrian glanced away. "Take her to my quarters."

"Yes, my lord."

They worked together to lift Ayleth's body off the saddle. Cassian cradled her in his arms and moved toward the front steps of the keep.

Gabrian used his last bit of magic for strength as he staggered toward his chambers. When he arrived, the door stood open, a fire crackled, and lanterns lit the room. Lenora must have heard him return and rushed to prepare it.

"Put her there." He pointed toward his bed.

Cassian laid Ayleth down and stepped back, his eyes full of tears. "I'm sorry, Gabrian. It's just so unthinkable."

"Yes. It's a terrible loss for us all."

"What's your command, sir?"

"Have hot water and fresh linens brought up."

Cassian nodded and hurried down the hallway.

Magic drained from Gabrian's hands, and he slumped in exhaustion. A knock on his door roused him. He groaned. "Yes?"

Lenora's voice echoed in the hallway. "Gabrian, I just heard. I'm so sorry. Here are more clean linens, and water is heating in the kitchen."

"Place them by the door."

The hallway was silent for several moments. "Sir? You should not be alone. Let me help."

"No, I'll take care of it."

"But, sir . . ."

"Instruct the guards to leave water buckets outside and not disturb me."

A sob erupted from Lenora's throat. "Can I at least come in to say goodbye?"

Gabrian paused. He had been too busy preparing his plan to consider that others would need to mourn. Lenora had practically raised Ayleth and felt the loss deeply. Even battle-hardened Cassian had tears in his eyes. What was it about Ayleth that created such devotion? All he had ever focused on was her studies and training her to use magic to help him return Algowin to power. But neither Cassian nor Lenora had seen any of that. She was simply the young woman who shared life with them. He was proud of Ayleth's accomplishments, but that wasn't the same. Maybe his approach had been a mistake, but it was too late for regrets.

"Of course. I'll send word to you once I have her prepared."

"Thank you." She sniffled and hurried down the hall.

He rubbed his eyes and glanced at the bundle on the bed. He stumbled over and unwrapped the cloak from Ayleth's body and cut away her tattered, muddy robe to reveal someone not quite human. A scaly pattern covered her body up to her throat. It flowed down her arms and legs, ending at her ankles and wrists. He brushed back dirty tendrils of hair, exposing the scales that framed her face. Her long, slender fingers and toes ended in claws.

He shook her shoulders and called her name. A rush of blood reddened her cheeks momentarily before turning pale again. If Ayleth were still alive, why didn't she wake up? Had the dragon pulled her down into a place somewhere near the edge of the underworld? He placed his fingertips on her temples and closed his eyes. A faint thread of magic circled her body like a cocoon. It contained her essence and fragments of the dragon. Her pulse was weak but steady, and her skin was cool. Her breathing was barely perceptible, but she was alive. By some miracle of the gods, the soul of the dragon captured in her chest kept her heart beating. They were now one, and Emelthedin's will to live belonged to them both.

What had gone wrong? What could he do to reverse the forced state of slumber? Of the five mages on his council, three were young and unskilled. Their combined strength would not be enough to revive her. He needed dragon magic, and the only place it might still exist was Dragonswold. He would send word to all his contacts in Sigor to listen for news from the Guardians and wait. In the meantime, he would ensure that Ayleth was placed in a safe location where she would not be disturbed.

A loud bang on the door told him that the buckets of water had arrived. "Leave them by the door."

"They're heavy, my lord. Are you..."

"I said leave them."

Wooden buckets scraped against the hallway's stone floor. When the sound of boots retreated, he opened the door and brought the buckets in with a pile of linen cloth and a tray of food.

He washed Ayleth as best he could and took the dirty linens and buckets of water out onto his balcony. He used one of his nightshirts to fashion a cover for her with slits in the back to fit around her wings and pulled heavy wool socks onto her feet, taking care not to snag them on her claws. Unclipping the brooch on his lapel that identified him as Lord of Algowin, he pinned it to the front of Ayleth's garment. He was not prone to sentimentality, but in case she woke up, he wanted her to know he had taken great care of her.

He wrapped her tightly in a silver shroud and secured it with silk cords, ensuring her wings were secure against her body. Later tonight, when everyone was asleep, he would move her to a place where he was sure she would be safe. The keep was ancient, built in the era when the mages of Algowin controlled dragons. And just like in Dragonswold, there had been a Dragonkeeper. A hidden room high above them, accessed by a long stairway, was his secret. The chamber at the top was too small for a full-grown dragon and had possibly been used to store eggs and other Dragonkeeper tasks. It was a fitting place for Ayleth to rest.

He sent a message to Cassian and Lenora to come to his chamber, and secured the shroud tightly around Ayleth's face, exposing only her eyes, nose, and mouth.

Shortly after, Lenora arrived and stood next to the bed.

"I'll give you a moment." Gabrian stepped into the hallway.

Cassian appeared from the stairwell and came to Gabrian's side. "My condolences, sir. May she rest with the gods."

Gabrian nodded. "Lenore is paying her respects. We'll wait here."

"Of course, sir."

"I need your help to carry her to the burial chamber."

"It will be my honor."

"But Cassian..."

"Yes."

"You must not disclose its location. Ever."

His brow creased, but he remained quiet.

"I trust no one else for this task. We must ensure Ayleth's final resting place remains undisturbed."

"As you wish, Gabrian. You have my word."

Lenora opened the door, dabbing tears from her eyes. "Thank you." She choked and disappeared down the hall.

Gabrian motioned for Cassian to enter, and they approached the bed. A small bouquet of marigolds and rosemary rested on Ayleth's breast. Gabrian set the flowers aside and gestured for Cassian to retrieve Ayleth's body.

He gathered her into his arms and waited.

Gabrian grasped a shoulder pack and water skein off the table, slung them over his shoulder, and stepped into the hallway. Down the tower's steps, Cassian trailed behind him to a door in a long, dark corridor that seemed to lead nowhere.

"Where to now, my lord?" he asked.

Gabrian stepped around him and touched the stone at the end of the hallway. A doorway appeared.

Cassian sucked in a breath and followed Gabrian through the door, which swung closed behind them.

The steep stone stairs that led them into the mountain gave no clue as to the time of day. The only illumination source was several mage lights bobbing along as they climbed. Starting just before midnight, it would take them until midday to reach the chamber.

Cassian continued without complaint until his breath tore from his chest, deep and ragged.

Gabrian pointed to a small alcove at the side of the tunnel. "We can rest here."Cassian placed Ayleth on the stone floor and stretched deeply with a groan. "How much longer, sir?"

"Hours, and we will continue to climb upwards. Let me know when you're rested enough to continue."

He took a long swig of water and rolled his shoulders. "Ready." He lifted Ayleth into his arms.

Gabrian noticed the subtle change in the stone walls as they moved higher into the mountain. As a young man, he climbed to the chamber but remembered little of the passages. Workers using chisels and hammers had roughly chipped the lower parts away. At the beginning, the tunnel was warm and stuffy. As they rose, the temperature chilled, and the walls smoothed. Mages with stone magic had joined to speed up the process. The walls glistened like marble, with the occasional magic symbol or signature to mark a particular alchemist's work.

Cassian focused on his task and remained oblivious to the surrounding changes.

After a long, smooth incline, they reached a set of stairs that rose steeply above them. Gabrian raised his hand for them to pause.

"This is the final set of stairs. Stop for a moment and catch your breath."

Cassian gently placed Ayleth down and leaned forward to look up the dark steps. "I've been here for twenty years and did not know this was here."

"That was not by accident. My father brought me here when I was young. I'm the only one still alive who knows it exists."

"Amazing," Cassian passed his hand over the smooth stone wall. "It must be as old as the keep itself."

"I'm certain it is. Are you ready to continue?"

"Yes, sir."

Gabrian shifted the bag on his shoulder and hastened up the stairs, disappearing into the dark.

Cassian pushed himself up the last several steps, wheezing. He stepped into the level corridor and stopped, his mouth agape. Images of battling dragons were carved along the hallway, twisting and turning in the air, spewing fire on the troops below. He turned slowly, gazing up and down the hallway, Ayleth still held in his arms. "What is this place?"

"It's so old, I have no records. But I believe it was a chamber for the Dragonkeeper of Algowin."

Cassian's eyes followed the hallway to where it ended at a large metal door, and his jaw dropped again. Two carved images stood guard on either side: a dragon on the left and a tall woman in a cloak on the right. "Who is that?"

"I'm uncertain. Perhaps the Dragonkeeper of Algowin was a woman."

The heavy doors creaked open, and they stepped into a large, rectangular room carved out of the side of the mountain. On the right, there were double doors. Freezing air seeped in around its edges. The room lacked decoration except for hammered metalwork on the hinges and door clasps.

"Bring her here." Gabrian pulled a wool blanket from his pack and spread it out in the middle of the room.

Cassian placed Ayleth's body in the center and wrapped it around her. He stood stiffly and wrapped his arms around his chest. "Brr," he pointed toward the doors. "Where do those go?"

"Open them and see," Gabrian fussed to tighten the blanket around Ayleth.

Cassian struggled with the rusted locks, and finally, the two doors swung open.

"Whoa," he peered down. "By the gods, we're at the top of the mountain."

Gabrian stepped behind Cassian and clasped his shoulder, preventing him from stepping away from the edge.

Cassian's back stiffened. "Sir?"

"You understand that the location of this room can never be revealed?" Gabrian asked.

"You've known me a long time." Cassian eyed the steep drop. "Is my word not good enough?"

Gabrian waited a few moments before releasing his grip and moving aside so Cassian could step back into the room.

"Good. I need a few moments alone before we go."

Cassian nodded crisply and left the room.

Gabrian locked the double doors tightly before returning to Ayleth's side. He knelt to touch her forehead. Her skin was cool, but warmer than the air inside the chamber. He grimaced. Nothing had gone as planned. They stopped the king from claiming the dragons, but lost them as well. Ayleth had attempted to save something from the disaster unfolding on the battlefield and captured dragon magic at a terrible cost. Still, the ultimate prize had slipped from his hands, trapped in Ayleth's body and inaccessible. He had failed, and she was a prisoner to magic he had no power to control.

He cursed the gods and pounded his fist on the stone floor. Unless he could source a mage with dragon magic, he would lose the only person who had ever felt like family. Before she came, he had never wanted one. His parents had left him to the care of wet nurses and housemaids. He had no siblings and grew up much like Ayleth, alone in his room, playing with bones, rocks, and magic. His parents had been afraid of him, too.

A tear leaked from his left eye. He stood abruptly and wiped it away, berating himself for being weak. He hurried toward the door and glanced back briefly over his shoulder. His breath caught in his throat.

"Goodbye, Ayleth."

CHAPTER TEN

GABRIAN'S DILEMMA

G abrian spent his days scouring ancient texts for passages about dragon magic. Has anyone else ever merged with one? What happened to them? Could the spell be reversed? All believed Ayleth had perished, buried in the mountain in a private ritual. They assumed his isolation was because of grief. He dared not tell anyone that she had successfully captured a dragon's soul and lay in a deep slumber far above the keep. King Eldridge would come for her if he found out.

A tap on his door pulled him from the pile of old books and tomes on his worktable. Lenora was at his door with food and drink. She came in carrying a tray and frowned.

"You look terrible, Gabrian. When did you last sleep? I know you're upset about Ayleth, but ignoring your needs won't bring her back."

He motioned for her to put the tray on his side table. "You're right. I could use a bath and a stroll outdoors. Have some hot water brought up for me."

"Of course. Is there something else?"

A shuffling of feet in the outside hallway caught their attention.

Cassian appeared in the doorway.

"There's a messenger from Sigor to see you, sir."

Gabrian brightened. "Show him in." He shooed Lenora out.

A male figure clad in riding leathers stepped into the room.

Gabrian motioned the man toward a chair before the fire.

"What news?"

The man cleared his throat. "I've met with all my contacts, spent every coin you gave me on bribes, and nobody has heard or seen any dragons. At least no one will say."

"What about Dragonswold and the Guardians?"

"Everyone left alive after the battle has disappeared into the hills, taking their dead with them. Some old men, women, and children remain, but their soldiers were lost."

"No sightings of dragons over the mountains?"

"None, sir."

Gabrian gazed at the fire. *Was it possible that every dragon died in the battle? Had the Guardian's Dragonkeeper, Vynrith, let them all fight to their deaths?*

"There is something else, sir."

Gabrian shook his head and refocused on the man. "Yes?"

"Once the vultures and ravens had done their work, the Guardians cleared the battlefield of all the dragon bones."

"What?" Gabrian choked. "A bunch of old women, men, and children moved a mountain of bones? I thought the treasure hunters and scalpers had hauled them away."

"No one could get near them. A spell protected them. The Guardians loaded them onto wagons and carted them away. Not so much as a tooth left, and no one knows where they took them." He stared at Gabrian. "The field is now filled with grass. You can't even tell what happened there."

Gabrian stood, and the man stood too.

"Thank you for your report." Gabrian handed him a pouch of coins. "Keep your ears open and let me know if you hear anything significant."

"Yes, sir." The man nodded and hurried out.

Excited voices floated up from the dining hall below. Gabrian stood on his balcony and peered over the canyon to the mountains in the east. Temperatures were unseasonably warm. Snow had fallen meekly a few days ago and melted by nightfall, leaving the landscape brown and bleak. The weather reflected his lack of celebration.

This was the second Winter's Turn feast without Ayleth, and he was no closer to an answer. None of his scouts had uncovered any evidence of dragons. Even the young men he had sent to the battlefield to scour for remnants of bones had come back empty-handed. All that was left were broken bits of a dragon skull and a desiccated heart that sat in a chest locked away inside his study.

The tapping on his door became increasingly urgent.

"Gabrian. It's time to come down and start the festivities," Lenora said. "Are you ready?"

He sighed. He would go down, make an appearance, and leave, certain no one would notice his absence once the banquet and music began.

"I'll be right down."

He walked over to stand in front of a full-length mirror and stared at his reflection. Dark circles rimmed his eyes, and streaks of grey frosted his temples. Worry lines creased his forehead. He sighed and turned from the mirror. A slight tremor of magic vibrated the stone beneath his feet. He looked up. *Ayleth, I haven't forgotten you.*

A rich embroidered burgundy jacket with gold trim hung off the back of a chair. He donned the coat, brushed his hair, and placed several diamond and emerald rings on his fingers. Glancing again in the mirror, he pinned his signal of authority onto his lapel and patted it lightly. After all, he was Lord of Algowin and should act like it. Ayleth would expect nothing less. He took a deep breath, straightened his back, and strode out the door.

ABOUT THE AUTHOR

J.L. Henker is a writer, blogger, and host of the YouTube Channel: Women Fantasy Authors. She is a fantasy/sci-fi writer and has short stories published in several anthologies. She is an active member of Women Writing Other Worlds: An Alliance of Fantasy & Science Fiction Writers. Her career has included bookseller, used/rare book buyer, and bookstore manager. When not writing, you will find her playing with her granddaughter, hiking, baking, and perusing local thrift stores for treasures. She lives in northern California with her wife, Diane, and a ginger cat named Leo.

Find out more at https://jlhenker.com

BlueSky: https://bsky.app/profile/jlhenker.bsky.social
LinkedIn: https://www.linkedin.com/in/jlhenker/
Women Fantasy Authors YouTube Channel:
https://www.youtube.com/@womenfantasyauthors

Thank you for reading! If you enjoyed this book, please consider leaving an honest review. It helps other readers discover it and supports my work as an author. I appreciate your feedback!

NEXT IN DRAGONSWOLD WAR SERIES

Continue the story of Ayleth and her struggle with the Guardians to control dragon magic.

Available at all major online book distributors.

READ CHAPTER ONE - CAVE OF WHISPERS

A BLACKENED HEART

G ondomir touched his protruding cheekbones in horror. His brittle skin stretched taut and pale. Blue veins twined up his arms, coursing blood toward his weakened heart. He clutched his throat and gasped for air, stretching a trembling arm towards his nightstand to reach a brass handbell. Shaking uncontrollably, he knocked it to the ground with a rattling clang. "Brenna," he whispered.

His chamber door opened, and a scowling woman entered. "What is the..." she gasped.

"Gondomir, by the gods, what happened?"

He struggled to speak. "I slept...help me."

She rushed to his side and helped him stand. Leaning heavily on her arm, he shuffled to a stone door at the back of his chamber. She whispered a chain of ancient words, the lock clicked open, and they entered a cramped, dark room. The air was stuffy and acrid, the walls stained with smoke. Gondomir wheezed and slumped into a heavy oaken chair.

Brenna brushed a tangled strand of hair away from his eyes. "I'll get it."

"Hurry." He slumped and gasped for air.

A wooden chest sat in the corner. She lifted the lid, grimaced, and pulled out an oblong item enshrouded in black silk. It was grotesque, and she hated to touch it. She set it on the table at Gabrian's side and returned to the chest to collect a silver goblet and a vial of black liquid. She lined up the items next to Gondomir and stepped back. He unfolded the silk, exposing a desiccated piece of flesh, the last bits of a dragon heart. He groaned and set it on the table, carefully cutting off a tiny piece and placing it in the goblet. The sliced pieces became smaller and smaller as he grew terrified of using the last. Why were the effects that used to prolong his youth for a hundred years only lasting several moon cycles? Perhaps the magic had faded over the centuries. Whatever it was, he was running out of time. If he wished to sustain his centuries-old body, he needed to draw energy from something living. Soon.

The rank liquid sizzled and popped as he poured it over the piece of heart. An acrid, foul smoke escaped into the chamber. He chanted in the ancient tongue, the bits and pieces dissolving in his bitter brew. Lifting the goblet with quivering hands, he raised it to his lips and drank several swift gulps. He pitched back in his chair, his arms and legs rigid, and the cup crashed to the floor. Within moments, his limbs softened, and his head fell forward onto his chest.

Brenna watched, as she had many times before, in horrified amazement as Gondomir's hair grew thick and dark and the lines in his face softened. His muscles filled out, and the skin covering his wasted bones returned to its youthful glow. His assistant for many years, she was still mystified by the magic he drew from the heart. Whatever its secrets, they were worth a mountain of gold. She would keep him alive to share in its wealth and power. "Let me help you to your bed."

He nodded and took her hand. "I'll rest for a few days. But not for long. The Council needs to prepare."

"Are they ready?"

"No. But we can't wait much longer. The last piece will be in place soon."

Brenna nodded. "What have you discovered from your spies in Sigor?"

"The mage we discovered is unhappy and restless. If she doesn't arrive on her own, I'll send a formal invitation."

"What makes you think she'll come?"

"The promise of power and a desire to resurrect a dragon."

Brenna nodded. "And if she doesn't come willingly?"

He smirked. "I'll bring her here myself."

Chairs scraped the floor, and robes rustled as the mages of Algowin waited for Gondomir to arrive in the council chamber. They assumed he was in seclusion for reflection and contemplation. It was not uncommon for him to disappear for days. They marveled at how refreshed and energetic he appeared after his chosen time alone—almost younger. Gondomir entered and greeted everyone as he made his way to the head of the table. He was confident in his standing. The mages around this table owed allegiance to him. All except Cynwold. The old man sat stooped in the chair to his right, scowling. When he arrived to reclaim it, Gondomir had found the scraggly mage squatting in his family's abandoned keep. Discovering Cynwold had served many years in the king's palace, knew ancient history, and had significant magical powers, Gondomir invited him to stay.

Sonlin sat by Cynwold. Gabrian's men snatched him from prison at Sigor. His crime? Impregnating a wealthy merchant's daughter and attempting to run away with her. The price to free a King's Mage was high, the negotiations long and difficult, but Gondomir paid in precious gems and gold with assurances that Sonlin would never use his magic against the crown.

Celina, a middle-aged woman with wild hair who dressed like a merchant from the southern desert kingdom of Sorathan, sat to Gondomir's left. Glass beads woven into her braids sparkled in the candlelight and round silver earrings with dangles jingled when she moved. Previously a trader in Sigor, she was cunning and powerful, acquiring the goods Gondomir requested and removing any obstacles, human or otherwise. She fled to Algowin ahead of the king's guard, avoiding arrest for extortion.

Next to Celina was Cardoc, a middle-aged trader from the Western Isles. Pirate is a more accurate term. He looked weather-worn and grim despite the richly appointed robes that draped from his muscular shoulders. Gondomir snatched him off the gallows platform, where he awaited his fate for stealing from the king's ships.

They were free because of him. Each was chosen for their magic. Gondomir motioned for a servant standing behind his chair to bring a tray with a carafe of honeyed mead he imbued with magic to ensure their compliance. Another servant followed, placing a silver goblet next to each of them and filling it with the fragrant golden liquid. Gondomir waited until everyone had a full goblet at their side. "Councilors. I chose you, but you stayed. When I tell you what's before us, we'll toast our destiny. We're bound, and there's no turning back."

A chorus of mumblings and questions filled the room.

He silenced them with a glare. "Let me explain."

Celina looked up from her clasped hands and smirked. "It's about time."

Gondomir ignored her. "I promised dragon magic would return to our control but didn't tell you how. You know the history: mages and dragons stalemated at the end of the Great War, the dragons dead or dying, their Guardian allies decimated. The few mages left alive at Algowin scattered for safety. Only one mage stayed behind to be a vessel, to enslave the last living shred of dragon magic."

Celina glanced up and arched an eyebrow. "Ayleth? From the old stories?"

He nodded. "And she's here."

The room erupted. Impossible. What? Fairytales. Absurd!

Gondomir held up his hand for silence. "It's true. She slumbers in a room above us, captive in a spell between life and death, waiting to be awakened."

Cynwold turned and glared at Gondomir. "Why did you wait so long to tell us? Why the secrecy?"

"I wanted to be sure the time was right."

Celina gaped. "You want us to awaken a mage dormant for centuries and release an unknown, powerful entity who trapped a dragon?"

Gondomir nodded. "Yes."

Cardoc sniffed. "Is that wise?"

"We need her magic."

Sonlin jumped up and knocked over his chair. "We're waking up a six-hundred-year-old woman?"

Gondomir twitched. "Not exactly."

To be continued...

OTHER PUBLICATIONS

WWOW 2026 ANTHOLOGY

Some secrets are hidden in ruins . . . Some are inside us.

Available at all major online book distributors.

OTHER PUBLICATIONS (CONTINUED)

ANTIFA LIT JOURNAL - VOLUME ONE

"In times of tyranny, the voices of comedy and subversion ring the truest and most brave. This is a book for these times." Jason Brick

Available at all major online book distributors.